goat girls

ALSO BY FRANCESCA LIA BLOCK

Weetzie Bat

Beautiful Boys

Girl Goddess #9: *Nine Stories*

The Hanged Man

Dangerous Angels: *The Weetzie Bat Books*

I Was a Teenage Fairy

Violet & Claire

The Rose and The Beast

Echo

Guarding the Moon: *A Mother's First Year*

Wasteland

Francesca Lia Block

goat girls

HARPERCOLLINS*PUBLISHERS*

Goat Girls

Copyright © 2004 by Francesca Lia Block

Witch Baby copyright © 1991 by Francesca Lia Block

Cherokee Bat and The Goat Guys copyright © 1992 by Francesca Lia Block

Library of Congress Cataloging-in-Publication Data

Block, Francesca Lia.

Goat girls / Francesca Lia Block.— 1st ed.

v. cm.

New edition of two novels previously published separately: New York : Harper Collins, 1991 and 1992 respectively.

Contents: Witch baby — Cherokee Bat and the Goat Guys.

ISBN 0-06-059434-9 (pbk.)

I. Block, Francesca Lia. Witch baby. 2004. II. Block, Francesca Lia. Cherokee Bat and the Goat Guys. 2004. III. Title.

PZ7.B61945Go 2004   2003027146

[Fic]—dc22

Typography by Alicia Mikles

1 2 3 4 5 6 7 8 9 10

First Edition

goat girls

goat girls

witch baby

cherokee bat and the goat guys

witch baby

Upon Time

Once upon a time. What is that supposed to mean?

In the room full of musical instruments, watercolor paints, candles, sparkles, beads, books, basketballs, roses, incense, surfboards, china pixie heads, lanky toy lizards and a rubber chicken, Witch Baby was curling her toes, tapping her drumsticks and pulling on the snarl balls in her hair. Above her hung the clock, luminous, like a moon.

Witch Baby had taken photographs of everyone in her almost-family—Weetzie Bat and My Secret Agent Lover Man, Cherokee Bat, Dirk McDonald and Duck Drake, Valentine, Ping Chong and Raphael Chong Jah-Love, Brandy-Lynn Bat and Coyote Dream Song. Then she had scrambled up the fireplace and pasted the pictures on the numbers of the clock. Because she had taken all the pictures herself, there was no witch child with dark tangled hair and tilted purple eyes.

What time are we upon and where do I belong? Witch Baby wondered as she went into the garden.

The peach trees, rosebushes and purple-flowering jacaranda were sparkling with strings of white lights. Witch Baby watched from behind the garden shed as her almost-family danced on the lawn, celebrating the completion of *Dangerous Angels*, a movie they had made about their lives. In *Angels*, Weetzie Bat met her best friend Dirk and wished on a genie lamp for "a Duck for Dirk and My Secret Agent Lover Man for me and a beautiful little house for us to live in happily ever after." The movie was about what happened when the wishes came true.

Witch Baby's almost-mother-and-father, Weetzie Bat and My Secret Agent Lover Man, were doing a cha-cha on the lawn. In a short pink evening gown, pink Harlequin sunglasses and a white feathered headdress, Weetzie looked like a strawberry sundae melting into My Secret Agent Lover Man's arms. Dirk McDonald was dancing with Duck Drake and pretending to balance his champagne glass on Duck's perfect blonde flat-top. Weetzie's mother, Brandy-Lynn Bat, was dancing with My Secret Agent Lover Man's best friend, Coyote. Valentine Jah-Love and his wife, Ping Chong, swayed together, while their Hershey's-powdered-chocolate-mix-colored son, Raphael Chong Jah-Love, danced with Weetzie's real daughter, Cherokee Bat. Even Slinkster Dog and Go-Go Girl were dancing, raised up circus style on their hind legs, wriggling their rears and surrounded by their puppies, Pee Wee, Wee Wee, Teenie Wee, Tiki Tee and Tee Pee, who were not really puppies anymore but had never gotten any bigger than when they were six months old.

Under the twinkling trees was a table covered with Guatemalan fabric, roses in juice jars, wax rose candles from Tijuana and plates of food—Weetzie's Vegetable Love-Rice, My Secret Agent Lover Man's guacamole, Dirk's homemade pizza, Duck's fig and berry salad and Surfer Surprise Protein Punch, Brandy-Lynn's pink macaroni, Coyote's cornmeal cakes, Ping's mushu plum crepes and Valentine's Jamaican plantain pie.

Witch Baby's stomach growled but she didn't

leave her hiding place. Instead, she listened to the reggae, surf, soul and salsa, tugged at the snarl balls in her hair and snapped pictures of all the couples. She wanted to dance but there was no one to dance with. There was only Rubber Chicken lying around somewhere inside the cottage. He always seemed to end up being her only partner.

After a while, Weetzie and My Secret Agent Lover Man sat down near the shed. Witch Baby watched them. Sometimes she thought she looked a little like My Secret Agent Lover Man; but she knew he and Weetzie had found her on their doorstep one day. Witch Baby didn't look like Weetzie Bat at all.

"What's wrong, my slinkster-love-man?" Witch Baby heard Weetzie ask as she handed My Secret Agent Lover Man a paper plate sagging with food. "Aren't you happy that we finished *Angels*?"

He lit a cigarette and stared past the party into the darkness. Shadows of roses moved across his angular face.

"The movie wasn't enough," he said. "We have more money now than we know what to do with. Sometimes this city feels like an expensive tomb. I want to do something that matters."

"But you speak with your movies," Weetzie said. "You are an important influence on people. You open eyes."

"It hasn't been enough. I need to think of something strong. When I was a kid I had a lamp shaped like a globe. I had newspaper articles all over my walls, too, like Witch Baby has—disasters and things. I always wished I could make the world as peaceful and bright as my lamp."

"Give yourself time," said Weetzie, and she took off his slouchy fedora, pushed back his dark hair and kissed his temples.

Witch Baby wished that she could go and sit on Weetzie's lap and whisper an idea for a movie into My Secret Agent Lover Man's ear. An idea to make him breathe deeply and sleep peacefully so the dark circles would fade from beneath his eyes. She wanted Weetzie and My Secret Agent Lover Man to stroke her hair and take her picture as if they were her real parents. But she did not go to them.

She turned to see Weetzie's mother, Brandy-Lynn, waltzing alone.

Weetzie had told Witch Baby that Brandy-Lynn had once been a beautiful starlet, and in the soft shadows of night roses, Witch Baby could see it now. Starlet. Starlit, like Weetzie and Cherokee, Witch Baby thought. Brandy-Lynn collapsed in a lawn chair to drink her martini and finger the silver heart locket she always wore around her neck. Inside the locket was a photograph of Weetzie's father, Charlie Bat, who had died years before. The white lights shone on the heart, the martini and the tears that slid down Brandy-Lynn's cheeks. Witch Baby wanted to pat the tears with her fingertip and taste the salt. Even after all this time, Brandy-Lynn cried often about Charlie Bat, but Witch Baby never cried about anything. Sometimes tears gathered, thick and seething salt in her chest, but she kept them there.

As Witch Baby imagined the way Brandy-Lynn's tears would feel on her own face, she saw Cherokee Bat dancing over to Brandy-Lynn and holding a piece of plantain pie.

"Eat some pie and come dance with me and Raphael, Grandma Brandy," Cherokee said. "You can show us how you danced when you were a movie star."

Brandy-Lynn wiped away her mascara-tinted tears and shakily held out her arms. Then she and Cherokee waltzed away across the lawn.

No one noticed Witch Baby as she went back inside the cottage, into the room she and Cherokee shared.

Cherokee's side of the room was filled with feathers, crystals, butterfly wings, rocks, shells and dried flowers. There was a small tepee that Coyote had helped Cherokee make. The walls on Witch Baby's side of the room were covered with newspaper clippings—nuclear accidents, violence, poverty and disease. Every night, before she went to bed, Witch Baby cut out three articles or pictures with a pair of toenail scissors and taped them to the wall. They made Cherokee cry.

"Why do you want to have those up there?" Weetzie asked. "You'll both have nightmares."

If Witch Baby didn't cut out three articles, she knew she would lie awake, watching the darkness break up into grainy dots around her head like an enlarged newspaper photo.

Tonight, when she came to the third article, Witch

Baby held her breath. Some Indians in South America had found a glowing blue ball. They stroked it, peeled off layers to decorate their walls and doorways, faces and bodies. Then one day they began to die. All of them. The blue globe was the radioactive part of an old x-ray machine.

Witch Baby burrowed under her blankets as Brandy-Lynn, Weetzie and Cherokee entered the room with plates of food. In their feathers, flowers and fringe, with their starlit hair, they looked more like three sisters than grandmother, mother and daughter.

"There you are!" Weetzie said. "Have some Love-Rice and come dance with us, my baby witch."

Witch Baby peeked out at the three blondes and snarled at them.

"Are you looking for those articles again? Why do you need those awful things?" Brandy-Lynn asked.

"What time are we upon and where do I belong?" Witch Baby mumbled.

"You belong here. In this city. In this house. With all of us," said Weetzie.

Witch Baby scowled at the clippings on her wall. The pictures stared back—missing children smiling, not knowing what was going to happen to them later; serial killers looking blind also, in another way.

"Why is this place called Los Angeles?" Witch Baby asked. "There aren't any angels."

"Maybe there are. Sometimes I see angels in the people I love," said Weetzie.

"What do angels look like?"

"They have wings and carry lilies," Cherokee said. "And they have blonde hair," she added, tossing her braids.

"Clutch pig!" said Witch Baby under her breath. She tugged at her own dark tangles.

"No, Cherokee," said Weetzie. "That's just in some old paintings. Angels can look like anyone. They can look like mysterious, beautiful, purple-eyed girls. Now eat your rice, Witch Baby, and come outside with us."

But Witch Baby curled up like a snail.

"Please, Witch. Come out and dance."

Witch Baby snailed up tighter.

"All right, then, sleep well, honey-honey. Dream of your own angels," said Weetzie, kissing the top of her almost-daughter's head. "But remember, this is where you belong."

She took Cherokee's hand, linked arms with Brandy-Lynn and left the room.

Witch Baby, who is not one of them, dreams of her own angel again. He is huddling on the curb of a dark, rainy street. Behind him is a building filled with golden lights, people and laughter, but he never goes inside. He stays out in the rain, the hollows of his eyes and cheeks full of shadows. When he sees Witch Baby, he opens his hands and holds them out to her. She never touches him in the dream, but she knows just how he would feel.

Witch Baby got out of bed. She put the article about the radioactive ball into her pocket. She put her black cowboy-boot roller skates on her feet.

As she skated away from the cottage, Witch Baby thought of the blue people, dying and beautiful.

Devil City, she said to herself. Los Diablos.

Globe Lamp

Witch Baby passed the Charlie Chaplin
Theater that had been shut down a long
time ago and was covered with graffiti
now. The theater still had pictures of Charlie Chaplin
on the walls, and they reminded Witch Baby of My
Secret Agent Lover Man.

Someday me and My Secret will reopen this theater, she thought. And we'll make our own movies
together, movies that change things.

Witch Baby passed Canter's, the all-night coffee
shop, where a man with dirt-blackened feet and a
cloak of rags sat on the sidewalk sniffing pancakes in
the air. She only had fifty cents in her pocket, but she
placed it carefully in his palm, then skated on past
the rows of markets that sold fruits and vegetables,

almonds and raisins, olive oil and honey. The markets were all closed for the night. So was the shop where Weetzie always bought vanilla and Vienna coffee beans. But next to the coffee bean shop was a window filled with strange things. There were cupids, monster heads, mermaids, Egyptian cats, jaguars with clocks in their bellies, animal skulls; and lighting up all the rest was a lamp shaped like a globe of the world.

Witch Baby stood in front of the dust-streaked window, wondering why she had never noticed this place before. She stared at the globe, thinking of My Secret Agent Lover Man and the lamp he had told Weetzie about.

Then she opened the door and skated into a room cluttered with merry-go-round horses, broken china, bolts of glittery fabric, Persian carpets and many lamps. The lamps weren't lit and the room was so dark that Witch Baby could hardly see. But she did notice a gold turban rising just above a low counter at the back of the store. A humming voice came from beneath the turban.

"Greetings. What have you come for?" The voice was like an insect buzzing toward Witch Baby and she saw a pair of slanted firefly eyes watching her. A tiny man stepped from behind the counter. He smelled of almonds and smoke.

"I want the globe lamp," Witch Baby said.

The man shuffled closer. "My, my, I haven't seen one of my own kind in ages. You're certainly small enough and you have the eyes. But I wouldn't have recognized you in those rolling boots. Is that what we're wearing these days?" He looked down at his embroidered, pointed-toed slippers. "What have you come for?"

"The globe lamp," Witch Baby repeated.

"I wouldn't recommend the globe lamp. It's not a traditional enough abode. On the other hand, you may not want to be bothered with all those people rubbing the lid and whispering their wishes all the time. It gets tiresome, doesn't it, this lamp business? They don't understand that the really good wishes like world peace are just out of our league and those love wishes are such a risk. So the globe's a fine disguise, I suppose. No one bothering you for happily ever after. I understand, believe me; that's why I quit. The lamp business I'm in now is much less complicated."

"What time are we upon and where do I belong?" Witch Baby asked.

"This is the time we're upon." He blinked three times, shuffled over to the window, drew back a black curtain and reached to touch the globe lamp. Suddenly it changed. Where there had been a painted sea, Witch Baby saw real water rippling. Where there had been painted continents, there were now forests, deserts and tiny, flickering cities. Witch Baby thought she heard a whisper of tears and moans, of gunshots and music.

The man unplugged the lamp, and it became dark and still. He carried it over to Witch Baby and placed it in her arms. Because she was so small, the lamp hid everything except for two hands with bitten fingernails and two skinny legs in black cowboy-boot roller skates.

"Where do I belong?"

"At home," said the man. "At home in the globe."

When Witch Baby peeked around the globe lamp to thank him, she found herself standing on the sidewalk in front of a deserted building. There was only dust and shadow in the window, but somehow

Witch Baby thought she saw the image of a tiny man reflected there. Skating home, she remembered the lights and whispers of the world.

It was late when Witch Baby returned to the cottage and tiptoed into the pink room that Weetzie and My Secret Agent Lover Man shared. They lay in their bed asleep, surrounded by bass guitars, tiki heads, balloons, two surfboards, a unicycle, a home-movie camera and Rubber Chicken. My Secret Agent Lover Man was tossing and turning and grinding his teeth. Weetzie lay beside him with her blonde mop of hair and aqua feather nightie. She was trying to stroke the lines out of his face.

Witch Baby watched them for a while. Then she plugged in the globe lamp, took the article about the glowing blue ball out of her pocket, put it on My Secret Agent Lover Man's chest and stepped back into the darkness.

Suddenly My Secret Agent Lover Man sat straight up in bed. He shone with sweat, blue in the globe-lamp light.

"What's wrong, honey-honey?" Weetzie asked, sitting up beside him and taking him in her arms.

"I dreamed about them again."

"The bodies . . . ?"

"Exploding. The men with masks."

"You'll feel better when you start your next movie," Weetzie said, rubbing his neck and shoulders and running her fingers through his hair. "You and our Witch Baby are just the same."

My Secret Agent Lover Man turned and saw the globe lamp shining in a corner of the room.

"Weetz!" he said. "Where did you find it? What a slinkster-cool gift! It's just like one I had when I was a kid."

"What are you talking about?" Weetzie asked. Then she turned, too, and saw the lamp. "Lanky Lizards!" she said. "I don't know where it came from!"

Witch Baby wanted to jump onto the bed, throw back her arms and say, "I know!" But instead she just watched. My Secret Agent Lover Man, who didn't look at all like Witch Baby now, stared as if he were hypnotized. Then he noticed the article, which had slipped into his lap.

"Two glowing blue globes," he said, gazing from

the piece of paper to the lamp. "I'm going to make a new movie, Weetz. One that really says something. Thank you for your inspiration, my magic slink!"

Before she could speak he took her in his arms and pressed his lips to hers.

Witch Baby turned away. Although her walls were papered with other pieces of pain, although her eyes were globes, he had not recognized her gift. She did not belong here.

Drum Love

In the garden shed, behind a cobweb curtain, Witch Baby was playing her drums.

It was the drumming of flashing dinosaur rock gods and goddesses who sweat starlight, the drumming of tall, muscly witch doctors who can make animals dance, wounds heal, rain fall and flowers open. But it began in Witch Baby's head and heart and came out through her small body and hands. Her only audience was a row of pictures she had taken of Raphael Chong Jah-Love.

Witch Baby had been in love with Raphael for as long as she could remember. His parents, Ping and Valentine, had known Weetzie even before she had met My Secret Agent Lover Man, and Raphael had played with Witch Baby and Cherokee since they were babies. Not only did Raphael look like powdered chocolate, but he smelled like it, too, and his eyes reminded Witch Baby of Hershey's Kisses. His mother, Ping, dressed him in bright red, green and yellow and twisted his hair into dreadlocks. ("Cables to heaven," said his father, Valentine, who had dreads too.) Raphael, the Chinese-Rasta parrot boy, loved to paint, and he covered the walls of his room with waterfalls, stars, rainbows, suns, moons, birds, flowers and fish. As soon as Witch Baby had learned to walk, she had chased after him, spying and dreaming that someday they would roll in the mud, dance with paint on their feet and play music together while Cherokee Bat took photographs of them.

But Raphael never paid much attention to Witch Baby. Until the day he came into the garden shed and stood staring at her with his slanted chocolate-Kiss eyes.

Witch Baby stopped drumming with her hands, but her heart began to pound. She didn't want Raphael to see the pictures of himself. "Go away!" she said.

He looked far into her pupils, then turned and left

the shed. Witch Baby beat hard on the drums to keep her tears from coming.

Witch babies never cry, she told herself.

The next day Raphael came back to the shed. Witch Baby stopped drumming and snarled at him.

"How did you get so good?" he asked her.

"I taught myself."

"You taught yourself! How?"

"I just hear it in my head and feel it in my hands."

"But what got you started? What made you want to play?"

Witch Baby remembered the day My Secret Agent Lover Man had brought her the drum set. She had pretended she wasn't interested because she was afraid that Cherokee would try to use the drums too. Then she had hidden them in the garden shed, sound-proofed the walls with foam and shag carpeting, put on her favorite records and taught herself to play. No one had ever heard her except for the flowerpots, the cobwebs, the pictures of Raphael and, now, Raphael himself.

"When I play drums I don't need to bite or kick or break, steal Duck's Fig Newtons or tear the hair off

Cherokee's Kachina Barbies," Witch Baby whispered.

"Teach me," Raphael said.

Witch Baby gnawed on the end of the drumstick.

"Teach me to play drums."

She narrowed her eyes.

"There is a girl I know," Raphael said, looking at Witch Baby. "And she would be very happy if I learned."

Witch Baby couldn't remember how to breathe. She wasn't sure if you take air in through your nose and let it out through your mouth or the other way around. There was only one girl, she thought, who would be very happy if Raphael learned to play drums, so happy that her toes would uncurl and her heart would play music like a magic bongo drum.

Witch Baby looked down at the floor of the shed so her long eyelashes, that had a purple tint from the reflection of her eyes, fanned out across the top of her cheeks. She held the drumsticks out to Raphael.

From then on, Raphael came over all the time for his lessons. He wasn't a very good drummer, but he looked good, biting his lip, raising his eyebrows and moving his neck back and forth so his dreadlocks danced. For Witch Baby, the best part of the lessons was when she got to play for him. He recorded her on tape and never took his eyes off her. It was as if she were being seen by someone for the first time. She imagined that the music turned into stars and birds and fish, like the ones Raphael painted, and spun, floated, swam in the air around them.

One day Raphael asked Witch Baby if he could play a tape he had made of her drumming and follow along silently, gesturing as if he were really playing.

"That way I'll feel like I'm as good as you, and I'll be more brave when I play," he said.

Witch Baby put on the tape and Raphael drummed along silently in the air.

Then the door of the shed opened, and Cherokee came in, brushing cobwebs out of her way. She was wearing her white suede fringed minidress and her moccasins, and she had feathers and turquoise beads in her long pale hair. Standing in the dim shed, Cherokee glowed. Raphael looked up while he was drumming and his chocolate-Kiss eyes seemed to melt. Witch Baby glared at Cherokee through a snarl of hair and chewed her nails.

Cherokee Brat Bath Mat Bat, she thought. Clutch pig! Go away and leave us alone. You do not belong here.

But Cherokee was lost in the music and began to dance, stamping and whirling like a small blonde Indian. She left trails of light in the air, and Raphael watched as if he were trying to paint pictures of her in his mind.

When the song was over, Cherokee went to Raphael and kissed him on the cheek.

"You are a slink-chunk, slam-dunk drummer, Raphael. I didn't really care about you learning to play drums. I just wanted to see what you'd do for me—how hard you'd try to be my best friend. But you've turned into a love-drum, drum-love!"

"Cherokee," he said softly.

She took his hand and they left the shed.

Witch Baby's heart felt like a giant bee sting, like a bee had stung her inside where her heart was supposed to be. Every time she heard her own drumbeats echoing in her head, the sting swelled with poison. She threw herself against the drums, kicking and clawing until she was bruised and some of the drum-skins were torn. Then she curled up on the floor of the shed, among the cobwebs that Cherokee had ruined, reminding herself that witch babies do not cry.

After that day Raphael Chong Jah-Love and Cherokee Bat became inseparable. They hiked up canyon trails, collected pebbles, looked for deer, built fires, had powwows, made papooses out of puppies and lay warming their bellies on rocks and chanting to the animals, trees, and earth, "You are all my rela-tions," the way My Secret Agent Lover Man's friend Coyote had showed them. They painted on every sur-face they could find, including each other. They spent hours gazing at each other until their eyes were all pupil and Cherokee's looked as dark as Raphael's. No one could get their attention.

Weetzie, My Secret Agent Lover Man, and Valentine and Ping Chong Jah-Love watched them.

"They are just babies still," My Secret Agent Lover Man said. "How could they be so in love? They remind me of us."

"If I had met you when I was little, I would have acted the same way," Weetzie said.

"But it's funny," said Ping. "I always thought
Witch Baby was secretly in love with Raphael."

While Raphael and Cherokee fell in love, they
forgot all about drums. Witch Baby stopped playing
drums too. She pulled apart Cherokee's Kachina
Barbie dolls, scattering their limbs throughout the
cottage and even sticking some parts in Brandy-
Lynn's Jell-O mold. She stole Duck's Fig Newtons,
made dresses out of Dirk's best shirts and bit
Weetzie's fingers when Weetzie tried to serve her vegetables.

"Witch Baby! Stop that! Weetzie's fingers are not
carrots!" My Secret Agent Lover Man exclaimed,
kissing Weetzie's nibbled fingertips.

Witch Baby went around the cottage taking candid pictures of everyone looking their worst—My
Secret Agent Lover Man with a hangover, Weetzie
covered with paint and glue, Dirk and Duck arguing,
Brandy-Lynn weeping into a martini, Cherokee and
Raphael gobbling up the vegetarian lasagna Weetzie
was saving for dinner.

Witch Baby was wild, snarled, tangled and angry.
Everyone got more and more frustrated with her.

When they tried to grab her, even for a hug, she would wriggle away, her body quick-slippery as a fish. She never cried, but she always wanted to cry. Finally, while she was watching Cherokee and Raphael running around the cottage in circles, whooping and flapping their feather-decorated arms, Witch Baby remembered something Cherokee had done to her when they were very young. Late at night she got out of her bed, took the toenail scissors she had hidden under her pillow, crept over to Cherokee's tepee and snipped at Cherokee's hair. She did not cut straight across, but chopped unevenly, and the ragged strands of hair fell like moonlight.

The next morning Witch Baby hid in the shed and waited. Then she heard a scream coming from the cottage. She felt as if someone had crammed a bean-cheese-hot-dog-pastrami burrito down her throat.

Witch Baby hid in the shed all day. When everyone was asleep she crept back into the cottage, went into the violet-and-aqua-tiled bathroom and stared at herself in the mirror. She saw a messy nest of hair, a pale, skinny body, knobby, skinned knees and feet with curling toes.

No wonder Raphael doesn't love me, Witch Baby thought. I am a baby witch.

She took the toenail scissors and began to chop at her own hair. Then she plugged in My Secret Agent Lover Man's razor, turned it on and listened to it buzz at her like a hungry metal animal.

When her scalp was completely bald, Witch Baby, with her deep-set, luminous, jacaranda-blossom-colored eyes, looked as if she had drifted down from some other planet.

But Witch Baby did not see her eerie, fairy, genie, moon-witch beauty, the beauty of twilight and rainstorms. "You'll never belong to anyone," she said to the bald girl in the mirror.

Tree Spirit

The chain saws were buzzing like giant razors. Witch Baby pressed her palms over her ears. "What is going on?" Coyote cried, padding into the cottage.

Witch Baby had hardly ever heard Coyote raise his voice before. She curled up under the clock, and he knelt beside her so that his long braid brushed her cheek. She saw the full veins in his callused hands, the turquoise-studded band, blood-blue, at his wrist.

"Where is everyone, my little bald one?" he asked gently.

"They went to the street fair."

"And they left you here with the dying trees?"

"I didn't want to go with them."

Coyote put his hand on Witch Baby's head. It fit

perfectly like a cap. His touch quieted the saws for a moment and stilled the blood beating at Witch Baby's naked temples. "Why not?" he asked.

"I get lonely with them."

"With all that big family you have?"

"More than when I'm alone."

Coyote nodded. "I would rather be alone most of the time. It's quieter. Someday I will live in the desert again with the Joshua trees." He took a handkerchief out of his leather backpack and unfolded it. Inside were five seeds. "Joshua tree seeds," he said. "In the blue desert moonlight, if you put your arms around Joshua trees and are very quiet, you can hear them speaking to you. Sometimes, if you turn around fast enough, you can catch them dancing behind your back."

Coyote squinted out the window at the falling branches, the whirlwind of leaves, blossoms and dust.

"Now I'm going to do something about those tree murderers." He went to the phone book, found the number of the school across the street, and called.

"I need to speak to the principal. It's about the trees."

He waited, drumming his fingers. Witch Baby crept up beside him, peering over the tabletop at the sunset desert of his face.

"Is this the principal? I'd like to ask you why you are cutting those trees down. I would think that a school would be especially concerned. Do you know how long it takes trees to grow? Especially in this foul air?"

The saws kept buzzing brutally while he spoke. Witch Baby thought about the jacaranda trees across the street. Coyote had told her that all trees have spirits, and she imagined women with long, light-boned limbs and falls of whispery green hair, dark Coyote men with skin like clay as it smooths on the potter's wheel. Some might even be hairless girls like Witch Baby—the purple-eyed spirits of jacaranda trees.

Finally, Coyote put the phone down. He and Witch Baby sat together at the window, wincing as all the trees in front of the school became a woodpile scattered with purple blossoms.

Coyote is like My Secret and me, Witch Baby thought, feeling the warmth of his presence beside her. But he recognizes that I am like him and My Secret doesn't see.

Witch Baby's almost-family came home and saw them still sitting there. Weetzie invited Coyote to stay for dinner but he solemnly shook his head.

"I couldn't eat anything after what we saw today," he said.

That night, when everyone else was asleep, Witch Baby unfolded the handkerchief she had stolen from Coyote's backpack and looked at the five Joshua tree seeds. They seemed to glow, and she thought she heard them whispering as she crept out the window and into the moonlight. In the soil from which the jacaranda trees had been torn, Witch Baby knelt and planted Coyote's five seeds, imagining how one day she and Coyote would fling their arms around five Joshua trees. If she was very quiet she might be able to hear the trees telling her the secrets of the desert.

"Where are they?"

Coyote stood towering above Witch Baby's bed. She blinked up at him, her dreams of singing trees passing away like clouds across the moon, until she saw his face clearly. His hair was unbraided and fell loose around his shoulders.

"Where are my Joshua tree seeds, Witch Baby?"

Witch Baby sat up in bed. It was early morning and still quiet. There was no buzzing today; all the trees were already down.

"I planted them for you," she said.

Coyote looked as if the sound of chain saws were still filling his head. "What? You planted them? Where did you plant them? Those were special seeds. My Secret Agent Lover Man brought them to me from the desert. I told him I had to take them back the next time I went, because Joshua trees grow only on sacred desert ground. They'll never grow where you planted them."

"But I planted them in front of the school because of yesterday. They'll grow there and we'll always be able to look at them and listen to what they tell us."

"They'll never grow," Coyote said. "They are lost."

Witch Baby spent the next three nights clutching a flashlight and digging in the earth in front of the school for the Joshua tree seeds, but there was no sign of them. Her fingers ached, the nails full of soil, the knuckles scratched by rocks and twigs. She was kneeling in dirt, covered in dirt, wishing for the tree spirits to take her away with them to a place where Joshua trees sang and danced in the blue moonlight.

Stowawitch

It was Dirk who found Witch Baby digging in the dirt. He was taking a late-night run on his glowing silver Nikes when he noticed the spot of light flitting over the ground in front of the school. Then he saw the outline of a tree spirit crouched in the darkness. He ran over and called to Witch Baby.

"What are you doing out here, Miss Witch?"

Witch Baby flicked off the flashlight and didn't answer, but when Dirk came over, she let him lift her in his beautiful, sweaty arms and carry her into the house. She leaned against him, limp with exhaustion.

"Never go off at night by yourself anymore," Dirk said as he tucked her into bed. "If you want, you can wake me and we can go on a run. I know what it's like to feel scared and awake in the night. Sometimes I could go dig in the earth too, when I feel that way."

Before Witch Baby fell asleep that night she looked at the picture she had taken of Dirk and Duck at the party. Dirk, who looked even taller than he was because of his Mohawk and thick-soled creepers, was pretending to balance a champagne glass on Duck's flat-top and Duck's blue eyes were rolled upward, watching the glass. Almost anyone could see by the picture that Dirk and Duck were in love.

Dirk and Duck are different from most people too, Witch Baby thought. Sometimes they must feel like they don't belong just because they love each other.

When Dirk and Duck announced that they were going to Santa Cruz to visit Duck's family, Witch Baby asked if she could go with them.

"I'm sorry, Witch Baby," Dirk said, rubbing his hand over the fuzz that had grown back on her scalp. "Duck and I need to spend some time alone together. Someday, when you are in love, you will understand."

"Besides, I haven't seen my family in years," Duck said. "It might be kind of an intense scene. We'll bring you back some mini-Birkenstock sandals from Santa Cruz, though."

But Witch Baby didn't want Birkenstocks. And she already understood about spending time with the person you love. She wanted to go to Santa Cruz with Dirk and Duck, especially since she could never go anywhere with Raphael.

I'll be a stowaway, Witch Baby thought.

Dirk and Duck put their matching surfboards, their black-and-yellow wet suits, their flannel shirts, long underwear, Guatemalan shorts, hooded mole-man sweatshirts, Levi's and Vans and Weetzie's avocado sandwiches into Dirk's red 1955 Pontiac, Jerry, and kissed everyone good-bye—everyone except for Witch Baby, who had disappeared.

"I hope she's okay," Weetzie said.

"She's just hiding," said My Secret Agent Lover Man.

"Give the witch child these." Duck handed Weetzie a fresh box of Fig Newtons. He did not know that Witch Baby was hidden in Jerry's trunk, eating the rest of the Newtons he had packed away there.

On the way to Santa Cruz Dirk and Duck stopped along the coast to surf. They stopped so many times to surf and eat (they finished the avocado sandwiches in the first fifteen minutes and bought sunflower seeds, licorice, peaches and Foster's Freeze soft ice cream along the way) that they didn't get to Santa Cruz until late that night. Duck was driving when they arrived, and he pulled Jerry up in front of the Drake house where Duck's mother, Darlene, lived with her boyfriend, Chuck, and Duck's eight brothers and sisters. It was an old house, painted white, with a tangled garden and a bay window full of lace and crystals. In the driveway was a Volvo station wagon with a "Visualize World Peace" bumper sticker.

Dirk and Duck sat there in the dark car, and neither of them said anything for a long time. Witch Baby peeked out from the trunk and imagined Duck playing in the garden as a little Duck, freckled and tan. She imagined a young Duck running out the front door in a yellow wet suit with a too-big surfboard under one arm and flippers on his feet.

"I wish I could tell my mom about us," Duck said to Dirk, "but she'll never understand. I think we should wait till morning to go in. I don't want to wake them."

"Whatever you need to do," Dirk said. "We can go

to a motel or sleep in Jerry."

"I have a better idea," said Duck.

That night they slept on a picnic table at the beach, wrapped in sweaters and blankets to keep them warm. Duck looked at the full moon and said to Dirk, "The moon reminds me of my mom. So does the sound of the ocean. She used to say, 'Duck, how do you see the moon? Duck, how do you hear the ocean?' I can't remember how I used to answer."

When Dirk and Duck were asleep, Witch Baby climbed out of the trunk, stretched and peed.

I wish I could play my drums so they sounded the way I hear the ocean, she thought, closing her eyes and trying to fill herself with the concert of the night.

Then she looked up at the moon.

How do I see the moon? I wish I had a real mother to ask me.

The next morning, while Witch Baby hid in Jerry's trunk, Dirk and Duck hugged each other, surfed, took showers at the beach, put on clean clothes, slicked back their hair, hugged each other and drove to the Drake house.

Some children with upturned noses and blonde hair

like Duck's and Birkenstocks on their feet were playing with three white dogs in the garden. When Dirk and Duck came up the path, one of the children screamed, "Duck!" All of them ran and jumped on him, covering him with kisses. Then three older children came out of the house and jumped on Duck too.

"Dirk, this is Peace, Granola, Crystal, Chi, Aura, Tahini and the twins, Yin and Yang," Duck said. "Everybody, this is my friend, Dirk McDonald."

A petite blonde woman wearing Birkenstocks and a sundress came out of the house. "Duck!" she cried. "Duck!" She ran to him and they embraced.

Witch Baby watched from the trunk.

"We have missed you so much," Darlene Drake said. "Well, come in, come inside. Have some pancakes. Chuck'll be home soon."

Duck looked at Dirk. Then he said, "Mom, this is my friend, Dirk McDonald."

"I'm very happy to meet you, Mrs. Drake," Dirk said, putting out his hand.

"Hi, Dirk," said Darlene, but she hardly glanced at him. She was staring at her oldest son. "You look more like your dad than ever," she said, and her eyes filled with tears. "I wish he could see you!"

Dirk, Duck, Darlene and the little Drakes went into the house. Witch Baby climbed out of Jerry's trunk and sat in the flower box, watching through the window. She saw Darlene serve Duck and Dirk whole-wheat pancakes full of bananas and pecans and topped with plain yogurt and maple syrup. A little later the kitchen door opened and a big man with a red face came in.

"Chuck, honey, look who's here!" Darlene said, scurrying to him.

"Well, look who decided to wander back in!" Chuck said in a deep voice. He started to laugh. "Hey, Duck-dude! We thought you drowned or something, man!"

"Chuck!" said Darlene.

Duck looked at his pancakes.

"I'm just glad he's here now," Darlene said. "And this is Duck's friend . . ."

"Dirk," Dirk said.

"Do you surf, Dirk?" Chuck asked.

"Yes."

"Well, me, you and Duck can catch some Santa

Cruz waves. And I'll show you where the No-Cal babes hang," Chuck said.

"Chuck!" said Darlene.

"Darlene hates that," Chuck said, pinching her.

"Stop it, Chuck," Darlene said.

Witch Baby took a photograph of Duck pushing his pancakes around in a pool of syrup while Dirk glanced from him to Chuck and back. Then she climbed in through the window, hopping onto a plate of pancakes on the kitchen table.

"Oh my!" Darlene gasped. "Who is this?"

"Witch Baby!" Dirk and Duck shouted. "How did you get here?"

"I stowed away."

"I better call home and tell them," Duck said. "They're probably going crazy trying to find you." He got up to use the phone.

"Oh, you're a friend of Duck's," Darlene said as Duck left the room. "Well, stop dancing on the pancakes. You must be hungry; you're so skinny." She pointed at Witch Baby's black high-top sneakers covered with rubber bugs. "And we should get you some nice sandals."

Witch Baby thought of her toes curling out of a pair of Birkenstocks and looked down at the floor.

"They were worried about you, Witch Child," Duck said when he came back. "Weetzie bit off all her fingernails and My Secret Agent Lover Man drove around looking for you all night. Never run away like that again!"

Did they really miss me? she wondered. Did they even know who it was who was gone?

Duck turned to his brothers and sisters, who were staring at Witch Baby with their identical sets of blue eyes. "This is my family, Peace, Granola, Crystal, Chi, Aura, Tahini and Yin and Yang Drake," Duck said. "You guys, this is Witch Baby. She's my . . . she's our . . . well, she's our pancake dancer stowawitch!"

Witch Baby bared her teeth and Yin and Yang giggled. Then all Duck's brothers and sisters ran off to play in the garden.

Duck Mother

In Santa Cruz, Dirk, Duck and Darlene went for walks on the beach, hiked in the redwoods, marketed for organic vegetables and tofu and fed the chickens, the goat and the rabbit. Witch Baby followed along, taking pictures, whistling, growling, doing cartwheels, flips and imitations of Rubber Chicken and Charlie Chaplin and throwing pebbles at Dirk, Duck and Darlene when they ignored her. Sometimes, when a pebble skimmed her head, Darlene would turn around, look at the girl with the fuzzy scalp and sigh.

"Where did you find her?" she said to Dirk. "I've never seen a child like that." Then she would link arms with Duck and Dirk and keep walking.

"Mom, don't say that so loud!" Duck would say.

"You'll hurt her feelings."

But Witch Baby had already heard. She poked her tongue out at Darlene and tossed another pebble.

Clutch mother duck!

That evening, Dirk, Duck and Darlene were walking the dogs. Witch Baby was following them, watching and listening and sniffing the sea and pine in the air.

"Dirk, you are such a gentleman," Darlene said. "Your parents did a good job of raising you."

"I was raised by my Grandma Fifi," Dirk said. "My parents died when I was really little. I don't even remember them. They were both killed in a car accident."

Darlene's eyes filled with tears. "Like Duck's dad," she said.

That night she gave both Dirk and Duck fisherman sweaters that had belonged to Duck's dad, Eddie Drake. She didn't give Witch Baby anything.

Witch Baby kept watching and listening and nibbling her fingernails. She hid in the closet in Duck's old bedroom, with the fading surf pictures on the walls and the twin beds with surfing Snoopy sheets, and heard Duck and Dirk talking about Darlene's boyfriend, Chuck.

"He is such a greaseburger!" Duck told Dirk.

"Tell me about your dad, Duck," Dirk said. He had asked before, but Duck wouldn't talk about Eddie Drake.

"He was a killer Malibu surfer," Duck said. "I mean, a *fine* athlete. He had this real peaceful look on his face, a little spaced out, you know, but at peace. They were totally in love. She was Miss Zuma Beach. They fell in love when they were fourteen and, like, that was it. They had all of us one right after the other. Me while they were into the total surf scene when we lived in Malibu, Peace and Granola during their hippie-rebel phase, and then they got more into Eastern philosophy—you know, the twins, Yin and Yang. But then he died. He was surfing." Duck blinked the tears out of his eyes. "I still can't talk about it," he said.

"Duck." Dirk touched his cheek.

"I remember, later, my mom trying to run into the water and I'm trying to hold her back and her hair and my tears are so bright that I'm blind. I knew she would have walked right into the ocean after him and kept going. In a way I wanted to go too."

"Don't say that, puppy," Dirk whispered.

Witch Baby tried to swallow the sandy lump in her throat.

"But who the hell is Chuck?" Duck said. "I couldn't believe she'd be with a greaseburger like that, so I left. Plus, I knew they'd never understand about me liking guys."

Dirk kissed a tear that had slid onto Duck's tan and freckled shoulder and he drew Duck into his arms, into arms that had lifted Witch Baby from the dirt the night she had been searching for the Joshua tree seeds.

Just then, Witch Baby stepped out of the closet, holding out her finger to touch Duck's tears, wanting to share Dirk's arms.

"What are you doing here, Witch?" Duck said, startled.

"Go back to bed, Witch Baby," said Dirk, and she scampered away.

Later, curled beneath the cot that Darlene had set up for her in Yin and Yang's room, Witch Baby tried to think of ways to make Dirk and Duck see that she understood them, she understood them better than anyone, even better than Duck's own mother. Then they might let her stay with them and see their tears, she thought.

The next day Duck and Darlene were walking through the redwood forest. Witch Baby was following them.

"Duck!" Witch Baby called, "Do you know that all trees have spirits? Maybe your dad is a tree now! Maybe your dad is a tree or a wave!"

Duck glanced at Darlene, concerned, then turned to Witch Baby and put his finger on his lips. "Let's talk about that later, Witch. Go and play with the twins or something," he said, and kept walking.

"Duck, why did you go away?" Darlene asked, ignoring Witch Baby. "What have you been doing with your life?"

Duck told Darlene about the cottage and his friends. He told her about the slinkster-cool movies they made, the jamming music they played and the dream waves they surfed. The Love-Rice fiestas, Chinese moon dragon celebrations and Jamaican beach parties.

"You sound very happy," Darlene said. "Do you have a girlfriend to take care of you?"

"My friends and I take care of each other," Duck said. "We are like a family."

"That's good," said Darlene. "They sound wonderful. The little witch is a little strange, but I really like Dirk."

Just then Witch Baby jumped down on the path in front of Duck and Darlene. She was covered with leaves and grimacing like an angry tree imp.

"That's good," she said. "That you like Dirk. Because Duck likes Dirk a lot too. They love each other more than anyone else in the world. They even sleep in the same bed with their arms around each other!"

"Witch Child!" Duck tried to grab her arm, but he missed and she escaped up into the branches of a young redwood.

Darlene stood absolutely still. The light through the ferns made her blonde hair turn a soft green. She looked at Duck.

"What does she mean?" Darlene asked. And then she began to cry.

She cried and cried. Duck put his arms around her, but no matter what Duck said, Darlene kept crying. She cried the whole way along the redwood path to the car. She cried the whole way back to the house, never saying a word.

"Mom!" Duck said. "Please, Mom. Talk to me! Why are you crying so much? I'm still me. I'm still here."

Darlene kept crying.

Back at the house Chuck was barbecuing burgers. Dirk and the kids were playing softball.

"What is it, Darlene?" Chuck asked.

Darlene just kept crying. Dirk came and stood next to Duck.

"I'm gay," Duck said suddenly.

Chuck and all Duck's brothers and sisters stared. Even Darlene's sobs quieted. Dirk raised his eyebrows in surprise. Duck's voice had sounded so strong and clear and sure.

There was a long silence.

"Better take a life insurance policy out on you!" Chuck said, laughing. "The way things are these days."

"Chuck!" Darlene began to sob again.

"You pretend to be so liberal and free and politically correct and you don't even try to understand," Duck said. "We're leaving."

"Clutch pigs!" said Witch Baby. "You can't even love your own son just because he loves Dirk. Dirk and Duck are the most slinkster-cool team."

Duck ran into the house to pack his things, and Dirk and Witch Baby followed him.

A little while later they all got into Jerry and began to drive away.

"Wait, Duck!" his brothers and sisters called. "Duck, wait, stay! Come back!"

Darlene hid her ex-Zuma-Beach-beauty-queen face in her hands. Chuck was flipping burgers. Dirk looked back as he drove Jerry away but Duck stared straight ahead. Witch Baby hid her head under a blanket.

On the way home from Santa Cruz, Dirk and Duck stopped to walk on the beach. They were wearing their matching hooded mole-man sweatshirts. Witch Baby walked a few feet behind them, hopping into their footprints, but they hardly noticed her. It was sunset and the sand looked pinkish silver.

"There are places somewhere in the world where colored sparks fly out of the sand," Dirk told Duck, trying to distract him. "And I've heard that right here, if you stare at the sun when it sets, you'll see a flash of green."

Duck was staring straight ahead at the pink clouds in the sky. There was a space in the clouds filled with deepening blue and one star.

"I want to let go of everything," Duck said. "All the pain and fear. I want to let it float away through that space in the clouds. That is what the sky and water are saying to do. Don't hold on to anything. But I can't let go of these feelings."

"Let go of everything," Witch Baby murmured.

Dirk put his arms around Duck.

"How could she be with him?" Duck asked the sky.

"She must have been lonely," Dirk said.

"If I ever lost you, no amount of loneliness or anything could drive me into the arms of another!" Duck said. "Especially not into the arms of a greaseburger like Chuck!"

Witch Baby felt like burying herself headfirst in the sand. She knew that if she did, Dirk would not lift her in his arms like a precious plant, as he had done that night in front of the school. She knew that Duck would never share his tears with her now.

Dirk and Duck gazed at the ocean.

"How do you hear the water?" Dirk asked Duck.

Dirk and Duck and Witch Baby didn't arrive at the cottage for three days because they stopped to camp along the coast. The whole time Dirk and Duck ignored Witch Baby. She wished she had her drums to play for them so that they might understand what she felt inside.

When they got home, they smelled garlic, basil and oregano as they came in the door. They entered the dining room and Duck practically jumped out of his Vans. There at the table with Weetzie, My Secret Agent Lover Man, Cherokee and Raphael sat Darlene, Granola, Peace, Crystal, Chi, Aura, Tahini and Yin and Yang Drake.

Darlene didn't have tears in her eyes. She and Weetzie were leaning together over their candle-lit angel hair pasta and laughing.

"Duck!" Darlene leaped up and ran to him. "I need to talk to you."

Darlene and Duck went out onto the porch. The crickets chirped and there were stars in the sky. The air smelled of flowers, smog and dinners.

"Duck," Darlene said. "After you told me, I went to everyone—my acupuncturist, my crystal healer and my sand-tray therapist. Then I went for a long walk and thought about you. I realized that it wasn't you so much as me, Duck. My femininity felt threatened. I don't know if you can understand that, but that's how it was. I felt that if my oldest son rejects women, he's rejecting me. That somehow I made him—you—feel bad about women. Ever since your dad died, I've been so vulnerable and confused about everything."

"This is crazy!" Duck said. "You are such a beautiful woman. And how I feel about Dirk has nothing to do with your femininity. I love Dirk. It just is that way."

"I don't understand," Darlene said. "But I'll try. I am worried about your health, though."

"Everyone has to be careful," Duck said. "Dirk and I believe there will be a cure very soon. But we are safe that way, now."

"I love you, Duck," said Darlene. "And your friend Dirk is darling. Your father would be proud of you."

"I miss him so much," said Duck putting his arms around her. "But he's still guiding us in a way, you know? When I'm surfing, especially, I feel like he's with me."

Suddenly there was the click and flash of a camera and Duck turned to see Witch Baby photographing them.

A few days later, after Darlene and the little Drakes had left, Duck found a new photograph pasted on the moon clock. The picture on the number eleven showed Weetzie, My Secret Agent Lover Man, Dirk, Duck, Cherokee, Raphael, Valentine, Ping, Coyote, Brandy-Lynn and Darlene. Their arms were linked and they were all smiling, cheese. It looked as if everyone except Witch Baby were having a picnic on the moon.

Angel Wish

No one at the cottage paid much attention to Witch Baby when she got back from Santa Cruz. They didn't even mention how worried they had been when she had disappeared. Everyone was too busy working on My Secret Agent Lover Man's new movie, *Los Diablos*, about the glowing blue radioactive ball.

So Witch Baby skated to the Spanish bungalow where Valentine and Ping Chong Jah-Love lived. Raphael lived with them, but he was almost always at the cottage with Cherokee.

Wind chimes hung like glass leaves from the porch, and the rosebush Ping had planted bloomed different colored roses on Valentine's, Ping's and Raphael's birthdays—one rose for each year. Now there were white roses for Ping. Inside, the bungalow was like a miniature rain forest. Valentine's wood carvings of birds and ebony people peered out among the ferns and small potted trees. Ping's shimmering green weavings were draped from the ceiling. Witch Baby sat in the Jah-Love rain forest bungalow watching Ping with her bird-of-paradise hair, kohl-lined eyes, coral lips, batik sarong skirt and jade dragon pendants, sewing a sapphire blue Chinese silk shirt for Valentine.

"Baby Jah-Love," Ping Chong sang. "Why are you so sad? Once I was sad like you. And then I met Valentine in a rain forest in Jamaica. He appeared out of the green mist. I had been dreaming of him and wishing for him forever. When I met Valentine I wasn't afraid anymore. I knew that my soul would always have a reflection and an echo and that even if we were apart—and we were for a while in the beginning—I finally knew what my soul looked and sounded like. I would have that forever, like a mirror or an echoing canyon."

Ping stopped, seeing Witch Baby's eyes. She knew Witch Baby was thinking about Raphael.

"Sometimes our Jah-Love friends fool us," she said. "We think we've found them and then they're just not the one. They look right and sound right and play the right instrument, even, but they're just not who we are looking for. I thought I found Valentine three times before I really did. And then there he was in the forest, like a tree that had turned into a man."

Witch Baby wanted to ask Ping how to find her Jah-Love angel. She knew Raphael was not him, even though Raphael had the right eyes and smile and name. She knew how he looked—the angel in her dream—but she didn't know how to find him. Should she roller-skate through the streets in the evenings when the streetlights flicker on? Should she stow away to Jamaica on a cruise ship and search for him in the rain forests and along the beaches? Would he come to her? Was he waiting, dreaming of her in the same way she waited and dreamed? Witch Baby thought that if anyone could help, it would be Ping, with her quick, small hands that could create dresses out of anything and make hair look like bunches of flowers or garlands of serpents, cables to heaven. But Witch Baby didn't know how to ask.

"Wishes are the best way," said a deep voice. It was the voice of Valentine Jah-Love. He had been building a set for *Los Diablos* and had come home to eat a lunch of noodles and coconut milk shakes with Ping.

Valentine sat beside Ping, circling her with his sleek arm, and grinned down at Witch Baby. "Wish on everything. Pink cars are good, especially old ones. And stars of course, first stars and shooting stars. Planes will do if they are the first light in the sky and look like stars. Wish in tunnels, holding your breath and lifting your feet off the ground. Birthday candles. Baby teeth."

Valentine showed his teeth, which were bright as candles. Then he got up and slipped the sapphire silk shirt over his dark shoulders.

"Even if you get your wish, there are usually complications. I wished for Ping Chong, but I didn't know we'd have so many problems in the world, from our families and even the ones we thought were our friends, just because my skin is dark and she is the color of certain lilies. But still you must wish." He looked at Ping. "I think Witch Baby might just find her angel on the set of *Los Diablos*," he said, pulling a tiny pink Thunderbird out of his trouser pocket. It came rolling toward Witch Baby through the tunnel Valentine made with his hand.

Niña Bruja

On the set of *Los Diablos*, My Secret Agent Lover Man and Weetzie sat in their canvas chairs, watching a group of dark children gathered in a circle around a glowing blue ball. Valentine was putting some finishing touches on a hut he had built. Ping was painting some actors glossy blue. Dirk and Duck were in the office making phone calls and looking at photos.

Witch Baby went to the set of *Los Diablos* to hide costumes, break light bulbs and throw pebbles at everyone. That was when she saw Angel Juan Perez for the first time.

But it wasn't really the first time. Witch Baby had dreamed about Angel Juan before she ever saw him. He had been the dark angel boy in her dream.

When the real Angel Juan saw Witch Baby watching him from behind My Secret Agent Lover Man's director's chair, he did the same thing that the dream Angel Juan had done—he stretched out his arms and opened his hands. She sent Valentine's pink Thunderbird rolling toward his feet and ran away.

"Niña Bruja!" Angel Juan called. "I've heard about you. Come back here!"

But she was already gone.

The next day Witch Baby watched Angel Juan on the set again. Coyote was covering Angel Juan's face with blue shavings from the sacred ball. They sat in the dark and Angel Juan's blue face glowed.

When the scene was over, Angel Juan found Witch Baby hiding behind My Secret Agent Lover Man's chair again.

"Come with me, Niña Bruja," he said, holding out his hand.

Witch Baby crossed her arms on her chest and stuck out her chin. Angel Juan shrugged, but when he skateboarded away she followed him on her roller skates. Soon they were rolling along side by side on the way to the cottage.

They climbed up a jacaranda tree in the garden and sat in the branches until their hair was covered with purple blossoms; climbed down and slithered through the mud, pretending to be seeds. They sprayed each other with the hose, and the water caught sunlight so that they were rinsed in showers of liquid rainbows. In the house they ate banana and peanut butter sandwiches, put on music and pretended to surf on Witch Baby's bed under the newspaper clippings.

"Where are you from, Angel Juan?" Witch Baby asked.

"Mexico."

Witch Baby had seen sugar skulls and candelabras in the shapes of doves, angels and trees. She had seen white dresses embroidered with gardens, and she had seen paintings of a dark woman with parrots and flowers and blood and one eyebrow. She liked tortillas with butter melting in the fold almost as much as candy, and she liked hot days and hibiscus flowers, mariachi bands and especially, now, Angel Juan.

Angels in Mexico might all have black hair,

Witch Baby thought. I might belong there.

"What's it like?" she asked, thinking of rose-covered saints and fountains.

"Where I'm from it's poor. Little kids sit on the street asking for change. Some of them sing songs and play guitars they've made themselves, or they sell rainbow wish bracelets. There are old ladies too—just sitting in the dirt. People come from your country with lots of money and fancy clothes. They go down to the bars, shoot tequila and go back up to buy things. It's crazy to see them leaving with their paper flowers and candles and blankets and stuff, like we have something they need, when most of us don't even have a place to sleep or food to eat. Maybe they just want to come see how we live to feel better about their lives, or maybe they're missing something else that we have. But you're different." He stared at Witch Baby. "Where did you come from?"

Witch Baby shrugged.

"Niña Bruja! Witch Baby! Cherokee and Raphael told me about you. What a crazy name! Why do they call you that? I don't think you're witchy at all."

"I don't know why."

"Who are your parents?"

Witch Baby shrugged again. She thought Angel Juan's eyes were like night houses because of the windows shining in them.

He sat watching her for a long time. Then he looked up at her wall with the newspaper clippings and said, "You need to find out. That would help. I bet you wouldn't need all these stories on your wall if you knew who you were."

Witch Baby took out her camera and looked at Angel Juan through the lens. "Can I?" she asked.

"Sure. Then I've got to go." Angel Juan winked at the camera and slid out the window. "*Adios*, Baby."

But Angel Juan came back. He and Witch Baby sat in the branches of the tree, whistling and chirping like birds. They went into the shed and he played My Secret Agent Lover Man's bass while Witch Baby jammed on the drums she hadn't touched for so long. Fireworks went off inside of her. Their lights came out through her eyes and shone on Angel Juan.

How could I not play? she wondered.

"They should call you Bongo Baby," Angel Juan said. "What does it feel like?"

"All the feelings that fly around in me like bats come together, hang upside down by their toes, fold up their wings, and stop flapping and there's just the music. No bat feelings. But sometimes the bats flap around so much that I can't play at all."

"Don't let them," said Angel Juan. "Never stop playing."

They made up songs like "Tijuana Surf," "Witch Baby Wiggle," and "Rocket Angel," and sometimes they put on music and danced—holding hands, jumping up and down, hiphopping, shimmying, spinning and swimming the air. They went to the tiny apartment where Angel Juan lived with his parents, Gabriela and Marquez Perez, and his brothers and sisters—Angel Miguel, Angel Pedro, Angelina and Serafina—and played basketball until it got dark, then went inside for fresh tortillas and salsa. The apartment was full of the lace doilies Gabriela crocheted. They looked like pressed roses covered with frost, like shadows or webs or clouds. Hanging on the walls and stacked on the floor were the picture frames that Marquez made. Some were simple wood, others were painted with blue roses and gold leaves; there were elaborately carved ones with angels at the four corners. Angel Juan and his brothers and sisters had drawn pictures to put in some of the frames, but most were empty. Everyone in the Perez family liked to hold the frames up around their faces and pretend to be different paintings. The first time Witch Baby came over and held up a frame, Angel Juan's brothers and sisters laughed in their high bird voices. They squealed at her hair and her name and her toes, but they always laughed at everyone and everything, including themselves, so she laughed too.

"Take our picture, Niña Bruja!" they chirped from inside one of Marquez's frames when they saw her camera.

The pictures of Angel Juan were always just a dark blur.

"Why do you move so fast?" she asked him. "You are even faster than I am."

"I'm always running away. Come on!" He took Witch Baby's hand and they flew down the street.

They flew. It felt like that. It was like having an angel for your best friend. An angel with black, black electric hair. It didn't even matter to Witch Baby that she didn't know who she was. At night she put pictures of an Angel Juan blur on her wall before she fell asleep.

Weetzie smiled when she saw the pictures. "Witch Baby is in love," she told My Secret Agent Lover Man. "Maybe she'll stop being obsessed with all those accidents and disasters, all that misery. It's too much for anyone, especially a child."

"Witchy plus Angel Juan!" Cherokee sang from inside her tepee. "Witch hasn't put up one scary picture for two weeks."

Witch Baby ignored Cherokee. She was wearing a T-shirt Angel Juan had given to her. Gabriela Perez had embroidered it with rows of tiny animals and it smelled like Angel Juan—like fresh, warm cornmeal and butter. The smell wrapped around Witch Baby as she drifted to sleep.

"My pain is ugly, Angel Juan. I feel like I have so much ugly pain," says Witch Baby in a dream.

"Everyone does," Angel Juan says. "My mother says that pain is hidden in everyone you see. She says try to imagine it like big bunches of flowers that everyone is

carrying around with them. Think of your pain like a big bunch of red roses, a beautiful thorn necklace. Everyone has one."

Witch Baby and Angel Juan made gardens of worlds. They were Gypsies and Indians, flamenco dancers and fauns. They were magicians, tightrope walkers, clowns, lions and elephants—a whole circus. They spun My Secret Agent Lover Man's globe lamp and went wherever their fingers landed.

"We live in a globe house."

"Our house is a globe."

"I am a Sphinx."

"I am a bullfighter who sets the bulls free."

"I am an African drummer dancing with a drum that is bigger than I am."

"I am a Hawaiian surfer with wreaths of leaves on my head and ankles."

"I am a dancing goddess with lots of arms."

"I am a Buddha."

"I am a painter from Mexico with parrots on my shoulders and a necklace of roses."

And then one day Angel Juan wasn't on the set of *Los Diablos*, where Witch Baby always met him.

Somehow she knew right away that something was wrong. She hurled herself past Dirk and Duck's trailer, among the children Ping was painting, under the radiant blue archways that Valentine was building. The whole set and everyone on it seemed to pulse with blue, the blue of fear, the blue of sorrow.

"Angel Juan!" Witch Baby called. She jumped up and down at Valentine's feet. "Have you seen Angel Juan?"

Valentine shook his head.

"Angel Juan!" cried Witch Baby, tugging at Ping's sarong.

"I haven't seen him today, Baby Love," said Ping.

Dirk and Duck opened the door of their trailer. They didn't know where Angel Juan was either.

My Secret Agent Lover Man was directing the scene in which Coyote was dying of radiation in a candle-lit room. Witch Baby pulled on the leg of My Secret Agent Lover Man's baggy trousers with her teeth.

"Cut!" he said.

Coyote sat up and opened his eyes.

My Secret Agent Lover Man scowled. "I'm busy now, Witch Baby. This is a very important scene. What do you want?"

"Angel Juan!"

"Angel Juan didn't come to the set today. I don't know where he is."

Witch Baby put on her skates and rolled away from the blue faces and archways as fast as she could. When she got to the Perez apartment, she felt as if a necklace of thorns had suddenly wrapped around her, pricking into her flesh.

Angel Juan was not there.

Angel Miguel, Angel Pedro, Angelina and Serafina were not playing basketball in the driveway. There weren't any baking smells coming from Gabriela's kitchen and there was no sound of Marquez's hammering. There was only a "For Rent" sign on the front lawn.

"Angel Juan!"

Witch Baby pressed her face against a window. The apartment was dark, with a few frames and doilies scattered on the floor, as if the Perez family had left in a hurry.

"I'm always running away," Angel Juan had said. Witch Baby heard his voice in her head as she skated home, stumbling into fences and tearing her skin on thorns.

Weetzie was talking on the phone and biting her fingernails when Witch Baby got there.

"Witch Baby!" she called, hanging up. "Come here, honey-honey!" She followed Witch Baby into her room and sat beside her on the bed while Witch Baby pulled off her roller skates.

"Where is Angel Juan?" Witch Baby demanded. On her wall the pictures of Angel Juan were all running away—blurs of black hair and white teeth.

Weetzie held out her arms to Witch Baby.

"Where is Angel Juan?"

"I just got a call from My Secret Agent Lover Man. He found out that the immigration officers were looking for the Perez family because they weren't supposed to be here anymore. They went back to Mexico."

Witch Baby leaped off the bed and out the window.

She wanted to run and run forever, until she

reached the border. She imagined it as an endless row of dark angel children with wish bracelets in their hands and thorns around their necks, sitting in the dirt and singing behind barbed wire.

My Secret

Witch Baby was crying. Witch babies never cry, snapped a voice inside, but she couldn't stop. Angel Juan had been gone for two days.

Weetzie had never seen Witch Baby cry before and went to hug her, but Witch Baby curled up like a snail in the corner of the bed, burying her face in the embroidered animal T-shirt Angel Juan had given her. It hardly smelled like him anymore. Weetzie saw that the tears streaking Witch Baby's face were the same color as her eyes.

"Come on," Weetzie said, scooping her up.

Because Witch Baby was limp from the tears and the effort of trying to find Angel Juan in the T-shirt, her kicks and kitten bites did not prevent Weetzie from carrying her into the pink bedroom.

My Secret Agent Lover Man was in bed, reading the paper. He had never seen Witch Baby cry before either.

"What is it?" he asked gently, moving aside so Weetzie and Witch Baby could sit on the warm place. He reached out to stroke Witch Baby's tangles, but she shrank away from him, baring her teeth and clinging to the T-shirt.

"She wants to understand about Angel Juan," Weetzie said. "I thought you could explain."

My Secret Agent Lover Man scratched his chin.

"The Perez family came here to work, to make beautiful things. But our government says they don't belong here and sent them back again. It doesn't make a lot of sense. I'm sorry, Witch Baby. I wish there was something I could do. Maybe with my movies, at least."

"Angel Juan belongs anywhere he is," Witch Baby said. "Because he *knows* who he is."

"He is lucky then," said My Secret Agent Lover Man. "And he will be okay."

"Will I see him again?" Witch Baby whispered.

"I don't know, Baby. There are barbed wire fences and high walls to keep the Perez family and lots of other people from coming here."

Witch Baby crawled under the bed and began to cry loud sobs that shook the mattress. She felt like a drum being beaten from the inside.

My Secret Agent Lover Man got down on his hands and knees and tried to reach for her, but she was too far under the bed. She looked at him through a glaze of amethyst tears.

"Who am I?" she asked, clutching Angel Juan's T-shirt to her chest. "I need to know. You tell me."

My Secret Agent Lover Man turned to Weetzie, who was kneeling beside him and she reached out and took his hand. Then he looked at Witch Baby again. His face was dusky with worry.

"I didn't want to tell you because I was afraid you would be ashamed of me," he began. "I'm sorry, Witch Baby. I should have told you before. See, I've always thought the world was a painful place. There were times I could hardly stand it. So when Weetzie wanted a baby, I said I didn't want one. I didn't want to bring any baby angel down into this messed-up world. It

seemed wrong. But Weetzie believed in good things—
in love—and she went ahead and made Cherokee with
Dirk and Duck. Or maybe Cherokee is mine. We'll
never be sure who her dad really is. Well, you know all
that.

"But then I got jealous and angry because of what
Weetz had done, so I went away.

"While I was away I met a woman. She was a powerful woman named Vixanne Wigg and I fell under her
spell. I didn't know what I was doing. Then something
happened that woke me up and I left. I found Weetzie
again, but I had been through a very dark time.

"One day Vixanne left a basket on our doorstep.
There was a baby in it. She had purple tilty eyes.

"The only good thing about what happened with
Vixanne Wigg was that we had made you, Witch Baby.
I didn't want to tell you about it because I wasn't sure
you would understand. But you're mine, Witch Baby.
Not only because I love you but because you are a part
of me. I'm your real father."

"And we all love you as if you were our real
child," Weetzie added. "Dirk and Duck and I. You
belong to all of us."

Witch Baby searched My Secret Agent Lover Man's face for her own, as she had always done. But now she knew. Tassellike eyelashes, delicate cheekbones, sharp chins. When he reached for her again, she let him bring her out from under the bed.

My Secret Agent Lover Man held Witch Baby against his heart, and she felt damp with tears and almost boneless like a newborn kitten. She closed her eyes.

She is holding on to the back of his black trench coat that has the fragrance of Drum tobacco from Amsterdam deep in the folds. His back is tense and bony like hers but his shoulders are strong. She is strong too, even though she is small—strong from playing drums—he has told her that. He will take her with him down arrow highways past glistening number cities, telling her stories about when she was a baby.

"My baby, my child that lay on the doorstep smoldering. For such a young child—it frightened us to see that strength and fire. But I knew you. I remembered the way I'd seen the world when I was young. I'd seen

the smoke and the pain in the streets, heard the roaring under the earth, felt the rage beneath the surface of everything, most people pretending it wasn't there. Only those who are so shaken or so brave can wear it in their eyes. The way you wear it in your eyes."

They are both dressed in Chaplin bowler hats and turned-out shoes as they ride My Secret Agent Lover Man's motorcycle around a clock that is a moon.

Witch Hunt

The next morning Witch Baby woke at dawn and ran around the cottage naked, crowing like a rooster and dragging Rubber Chicken along behind her. Cherokee climbed out of her tepee and stood in the hallway rubbing her eyes.

"Witch, why are you crowing?"

"My Secret Agent Lover Man is my real dad," Witch Baby crowed.

"He is not," Cherokee said. "I know! He and Weetzie found you on our doorstep."

"He told me he's my real dad! He went away and met my mom and she had me and brought me here."

"He is *not* your dad!"

"Yes he is. He's my real dad but maybe not yours. You'll never be sure who your real dad is!"

Cherokee began to cry. "My Secret Agent Lover Man and Dirk and Duck are all my dads. None of them are yours!"

"My Secret Agent Lover Man is," said Witch Baby. "You have three dads but it's like not having any. You're a brat bath mat bat."

Cherokee ran to My Secret Agent Lover Man and Weetzie's bedroom. Her face and cropped hair were wet with tears.

"Witch says I'm a brat mat because I have three dads!"

My Secret Agent Lover Man took her in his arms. "Cherokee, you've known about that all your life. Why are you so upset now?"

"Because Witch says you're her real dad. I want one real dad if she has one."

"Honey-honey," Weetzie said, "My Secret Agent Lover Man is Witch Baby's real dad, but you get to live with your real dad and two other dads even if you aren't sure which is which. Witch Baby doesn't even get to meet her real mom. Think what that must be like."

Cherokee stopped crying and caught a tear in her

mouth. She snuggled between My Secret Agent Lover Man and Weetzie, her hair mingling with Weetzie's in one shade of blonde.

None of them knew that Witch Baby was hiding at the doorway and that she had heard everything.

I'll meet my real mom! she told herself. I'll have two real parents and I'll know who I am more than Cherokee knows who she is.

The next morning Witch Baby put her baby blanket, her rubber-bug sneakers, her camera, Angel Juan's T-shirt and some Halloween candy she stole from Cherokee's hoard into her bat-shaped backpack, and she skated away on her cowboy-boot roller skates.

Later Weetzie and My Secret Agent Lover Man woke up and lay on their backs, holding hands and listening for the morning wake-up crow. But this morning the house was quiet and Rubber Chicken lay limply by the bed.

"Where is Witch Baby?"

They looked at each other, looked at the globe lamp on the bed table, looked at each other again and jumped out of bed. They ran through the cottage,

checking under sombreros and sofas, behind surfboards and inside cookie jars, but they couldn't find
Witch Baby. They woke Dirk and Duck, who were
surfing in their sleep in their blue bedroom, and told
them that Witch Baby was missing. Cherokee came
shuffling in, holding the puppy Tee Pee wrapped up
like a papoose.

Duck pushed his fingers frantically through his
flat-top. "I bet the witch child ran away!" he said.

Cherokee began to cry. "I've been so clutch to
her."

"Let's go!" Dirk said, pulling on his leather jacket
and Guatemalan shorts.

My Secret Agent Lover Man took the motorcycle,
Duck took his blue Bug, Dirk took Jerry, Weetzie
called Valentine and Ping who got in Valentine's VW
van. They drove in all directions looking for Witch
Baby. They went to the candy stores, camera stores,
music stores, toy stores and parks, asking about a
tiny, tufty-headed girl. Cherokee and Raphael ran to
Coyote's shack on the hill, chanting prayers to the sun
and looking in the muddy, weedy places that Witch
Baby loved. Brandy-Lynn stayed with Weetzie by the

phone, while Weetzie called everyone she knew and peeled the Nefertiti decals off her fingernails.

Weetzie and Brandy-Lynn waited and waited by the phone for hours. Finally, Weetzie's fatigue swept her into a dream about a house made of candy. Inside was a woman with a face the color of moss who warmed her hands by a wood-burning stove. A suffocating smoke came out of the stove and there was a tiny pair of black high-top sneakers beside it.

Weetzie woke crying and Brandy-Lynn held her until the sobs quieted and she could speak.

"Witch Baby is in danger," Weetzie said.

"Come on, sweet pea," said Brandy-Lynn. "I'll make you some tea. Chamomile with milk and honey like when you were little."

They sat drinking chamomile tea with milk and honey by the light of the globe lamp and Weetzie stared at the milk carton with a missing child's face printed on the back. She read the child's height, weight and date of birth, thinking the numbers seemed too low. How could this missing milk-carton child be so new, so small? Weetzie imagined waking up day after day waiting for Witch Baby, not knowing, seeing children's faces smiling blindly at her from milk cartons while she tried to swallow a bite of cereal. Seeing a picture of Witch Baby on a milk carton.

"Where do you think she could be?" Weetzie asked her mother. "Would she just run away from us? Last time she was with Dirk and Duck."

Brandy-Lynn was staring at the clock on the wall and the pictures Witch Baby had taken. There they all were—the family—bigger and bigger groups of them circling the clock up to the number eleven. They were all laughing, hugging, kissing. In one picture, Weetzie and Brandy-Lynn were displaying their polished toenails; in one, Weetzie and Cherokee wore matching feathered headdresses; Ping was playing with Raphael's dreadlocks; Darlene was messing up Duck's flat-top. There were pictures of My Secret Agent Lover Man, Dirk, Valentine and Coyote. But there was no picture on the number twelve.

"Look at all those beautiful photographs," Brandy-Lynn said. "And Witch Baby isn't even on the clock. No matter how much we love her, she doesn't feel she belongs. You have me, Cherokee has you, but Witch Baby still doesn't know who her mother is."

"I've been a terrible almost-mother," said Weetzie. "I won't just stop and pay attention when someone is sad. I try to make pain go away by pretending it isn't there. I should have seen her pain. It was all over her walls. It was all in her eyes."

"It takes time," Brandy-Lynn said, fingering the heart locket with the shadowy picture of Charlie Bat. "I didn't want to let you be the witch child you were once. I couldn't face your father's death. And even now darkness scares me." She set down the bottle of pale amber liqueur she was holding poised above her teacup, and pushed it away from her. "I didn't understand those newspaper clippings on Witch Baby's wall."

"How will I ever be able to tell Witch Baby what she means to us?" Weetzie cried. "She isn't just my baby, she's my teacher. She's our rooster in the morning, she's . . . How will I ever tell her?" she sobbed, while Brandy-Lynn stroked her hair. But Weetzie could not say the other thought. Would she be able to tell Witch Baby anything at all?

Vixanne Wigg

When she left the cottage, Witch Baby skated past the Charlie Chaplin Theater and the boys in too-big moon-walk high-tops playing basketball at the high school. She passed rows of markets where old men and women were stooped over bins of kiwis and cherries. They lived in the rest homes around the block, where ambulances came almost every day without using their sirens. One old woman with a peach in her hand stared as Witch Baby took her photograph and rolled away.

At Farmer's Market she skated past stalls selling flowers, the biggest fruits she had ever seen, New Orleans gumbo, sushi, date shakes, Belgian waffles, burritos and pizzas—all the smells mingling together into one feast. At the novelty store she saw pirate swords, beanies and vinyl shoppers covered with daisies. There were mini license plates and door plaques with almost every name in the world printed on them. But there was nothing with "Witch Baby" or "Vixanne" on it. Witch Baby knew she wouldn't find her mother here, eating waffles and drinking espresso in the sunshine. So she caught a bus to the park above the sea.

Under palm trees that cast their feathery shadows on the path and the green lawns, Witch Baby photographed men in ragged clothes asleep in a gazebo, and a woman standing on the corner swearing at the sun. Near the woman was a shopping cart packed with clothes, blankets, used milk cartons, newspapers and ivy vines. Witch Baby took a picture and put some of her Halloween candy into the woman's cart. Two young men were walking under the palms. They looked almost like twins—the way they were dressed and wore their hair—but one was tanned and healthy and one was fragile, limping in the protection of the other man's shadow over a heart-shaped plot of grass. Because of the palm trees, for a moment, the healthy man's shadow looked as if it had wings. Witch Baby took a picture and skated to the pier lined with booths full of stuffed animals.

She rode a black horse on the carousel, made faces at the mechanical fortune teller with the rolling eyeballs and bought a hot dog at the Cocky Moon. Nibbling her Cocky Moon dog, she stood at the edge of the pier and looked down at the blue-and-yellow circus tent in the parking lot by the ocean. Weetzie and My Secret Agent Lover Man had taken Witch Baby and Cherokee to the tent to see the clowns coming out of a silvery-sweet, jazzy mist. The silliest, tiniest girl clown hid behind a parasol and was transformed into a golden tightrope walker.

Witch Baby thought of the old ladies and the basketball boys, the street people and the clowns, the tightrope walker goddess and the man who could hardly walk. She remembered the globe lamp burning with life in the magic shop. She remembered Angel Juan's electric black-cat hair.

This is the time we're upon.

She skidded down to the sand, took off everything except for the strategic-triple-daisy bikini Weetzie had made for her and jumped into the sea.

Oily seaweed wrapped around her ankles and a harsh smell rose up from the waves, only partly disguised by the salt. Witch Baby thought of how Weetzie, My Secret Agent Lover Man, Dirk, Duck and Coyote had once walked all the way from town to bless the polluted bay with poems and tears. She got out of the water and built a sand castle with upside-down Coke cup turrets and a garden full of seaweed, cigarette butts and foil gum wrappers. Then she took pictures of surfer boys with peeling noses, blonde surfer girls that looked like tall Cherokees, big families with their music and melons, and men who lay in pairs by the blinding water.

When evening came Witch Baby had a sunburned nose and shoulders and she was starving. After she had eaten the sandy candy corn and Three Musketeers bars from her bat-shaped backpack, she was still hungry and it was getting cold.

I won't find my mother here, she thought, getting back on a bus headed for Hollywood.

She found a bus stop bench in front of the Chinese Theater and curled up under the frayed blanket in her backpack, the same blanket that had once covered her in the basket when Weetzie, My Secret Agent Lover Man, Dirk and Duck had found her on their doorstep. Shivering with cold, she finally slept.

The next morning Witch Baby waited until the tourists started arriving for the first matinee. She rolled backward, leaping and turning on her cowboy-boot skates over the movie-star prints in the cement all day, and some people put money in her backpack. Then she went to see "Hollywood in Miniature," where tiny cityscapes lit up in a dark room. Hollywood Boulevard was very different from the clean, ice-cream-colored miniature that didn't have any people on its tiny streets.

If there were people in "Hollywood in Miniature," they'd be dressed in white and glitter and roller skates, with enough food to eat and warm places to go at night, Witch Baby thought, watching some street kids with shaved heads huddling around a ghetto blaster as if it were a fire.

That was when she saw a piece of faded pink paper stapled to a telephone pole. The blonde actress in the picture pressed her breasts together with her arms and opened her mouth wide, but even with the cleavage and lips she looked small and lost.

"Jayne Mansfield Fan Club Meeting," said the sign. "Free Food and Entertainment! Candy! Children Welcome!" and there was an address and that day's date.

So Witch Baby ripped the pink sign from the telephone pole and took a bus up into the hills under the Hollywood sign.

Witch Baby skates until she comes to a pink Spanish-style house half hidden behind overgrown-pineapple-shaped palm trees and hibiscus flowers. Some beat-up 1950's convertibles are parked in front. Witch Baby takes off her skates, goes up to the house and knocks.

The door creaks open. Inside is darkness, the smell of burning wood and burning sugar. Witch Baby creeps down a hallway, jumping every time she glimpses imps with tufts of hair hiding in the shadows, and breathing again when she realizes that mirrors cover the walls. At the end of the hallway, she comes to a room where blondes in evening gowns sit around a fire pit roasting marshmallows and watching a large screen.

Their faces are marshmallow white in the firelight and their eyes look dead, as if they have watched too much television.

One of the women stands and turns to the doorway where Witch Baby hides. She is a tall woman with a tower of white-blonde hair and a chiffon scarf wound around her long neck.

"We have a visitor, Jaynes," the woman says.

Witch Baby feels herself being drawn into the fire-lit room. She stares into the woman's tilted purple eyes, a purple that is only found in jacaranda tree blossoms and certain silks, knowing that she has come to the right place.

"Are you Vixanne?"

"Who are you?" The woman's voice is carved—cold and hard. The necklace at her throat looks as if it is made of rock candy.

"Witch Baby Wigg, your daughter."

All the people in the room begin to laugh. Their voices flicker, as separate from their bodies as the shadows thrown on the walls by the flames.

"So this is Max's little girl. I wonder if she's as quick to come and go as her father was. Did Max and

that woman tell you all about how he left me, Witch Baby?" Vixanne asks. Then she turns to the people. "Do you think my daughter resembles me, Jaynes?" She reaches up and removes her blonde wig, letting her black hair cascade down, framing her fine-boned porcelain face.

"Let's see how my baby witch looks as a Jayne blonde," she says, putting the wig on Witch Baby. "You need a wig with that hair, Witch Baby!" The people laugh again.

"Now you can be a part of the Jayne Club." Vixanne leads Witch Baby over to the screen. Jayne Mansfield flickers there, giggles, her chest heaving.

"Sit here and have some candy," says someone in a deep voice, delicately patting the seat of a chair with two manicured fingers. Witch Baby can't tell if the thick, pale person in the wig and evening gown is a man or a woman.

Witch Baby sits up all night, gnawing on rock candy and divinity fudge, drinking Cokes, which aren't allowed at the cottage, and watching Jayne Mansfield films. After a while she feels sick and bloated from all the sugar. Lipstick-smeared mouths *loom around her. Her eyes begin to close.*

"I'll put you to bed now, Witch Baby Wigg,"
Vixanne says, lifting Witch Baby up in her powdery
arms.

There is something about being held by this
woman. Witch Baby feels she has fallen into an ocean.
But it is not an ocean of salt and shadows and dark-
jade dreams. Witch-Baby's senses are muffled by pale
shell-colored, spun-sugar waves that press her eyelids
shut, pour into her nostrils and ears, swell like syrup in
her mouth. A sea of forgetting.

Vixanne carries Witch Baby up a winding staircase
to a bedroom and tucks her beneath a pink satin com-
forter on a heart-shaped bed. Then she sits beside her
and they look at each other. They do not need to speak.
Without words, Witch Baby tells her mother what she
has seen or imagined—families dying of radiation,
old people in rest homes listening for sirens, ragged
men and women wandering barefoot through the city,
becoming ghosts because no one wanted to see them,
children holding out wish bracelets as they sit in the
gutter, the dark-haired boy who disappeared. What do
I do with it all? Witch Baby asks with her eyes.

Vixanne answers without speaking.

We are the same. Some people see more than others. It gets worse. I wanted to blind myself. You must just not look at it. You must forget. Forget everything.

And Witch Baby falls into a suffocating sleep.

In the morning, Witch Baby is too weak to get up. Vixanne comes in dressed in perfumed satin and carries Witch Baby's limp body downstairs. The others, the "Jaynes," are already gathered around the screen, eating candy and watching Jayne Mansfield waving from a convertible. Witch Baby sits propped up among them, wearing a long blonde wig. Her eyes are glazed like sugar cookies; her throat, no matter how many sodas she is given, is parched.

Late that night she wakes in her bed. "How will I ever be able to tell her what she means to us?" says a voice. Weetzie's voice. "Weetzie," she whispers.

She stumbles out of the room to the top of the stairs and looks down. Vixanne and the Jaynes are still watching the screen and charring marshmallows over the fire pit. A soft chant rises up. "We will ward off pain. There will be no pain. Forget that there is evil in the world. Forget. Forget everything." Vixanne is

*holding herself, rocking back and forth, smiling. Her
eyes are closed.*

*Witch Baby goes back into her room and packs her
bat-shaped backpack. For a moment she stops to look
at the pictures she has taken on her journey. The floating basketball boys. The old woman with the peach.
The hungry men in the gazebo. The dying young man
and his angel twin. A picture of a child with tangled
tufts of hair and mournful, tilted eyes. She leaves the
pictures on the heart-shaped bed, hoping that Vixanne
will look at them and see.*

*Then she slips downstairs, past the Jaynes and out
the front door. She sits on the front step, tying her roller
skates, clearing her lungs of smoke, gathering strength
from the night.*

*The mint and honeysuckle air is chilly on her
damp face, awake on the nape of her neck as Witch
Baby Wigg skates home.*

Black Lamb
Baby Witch

When Witch Baby tiptoed into the cottage, she saw Weetzie and My Secret Agent Lover Man holding each other and weeping in the milky dawn light. They looked as pale as the sky. She stood beside them, close enough so that she could feel their sobs shaking in her own body.

Weetzie lifted her head from My Secret Agent Lover Man's shoulder and turned around. Blind with tears, she held out her arms to the shadow child standing there. Only when Witch Baby was pressed against her, My Secret's arms circling them both, did Weetzie believe that the child was not a dream, a vision who had stepped from the milk-carton picture.

Beneath the pink feather sweater Weetzie was

wearing, Witch Baby felt Weetzie's heart fluttering like a bird.

"Will you tell everyone she's home? I need to be alone with her," Weetzie said to My Secret Agent Lover Man. She turned to Witch Baby. "Is that okay with you, honey-honey?"

Witch Baby nodded, and Weetzie put on her pink Harlequin sunglasses and carried Witch Baby out into the garden. The lawn was completely purple with jacaranda blossoms.

"Are you all right? We were so worried. Where did you go? Are you okay?" Witch Baby nodded, not wanting to move her ear away from the bird beating beneath Weetzie's pink feathers.

They were silent for a while, listening to the singing trees and the early traffic. Weetzie stroked Witch Baby's head.

"When I was little, my dad Charlie told me I was like a black lamb," Weetzie said. "My hair is really dark, you know, under all this bleach, not like Brandy-Lynn's and Cherokee's. I used to feel like I had sort of disappointed my mom. Not just because of my hair, but everything. But my dad said he was the black sheep of the family, too. The wild one who doesn't fit in."

"Like me."

"Yes," said Weetzie. "You remind me of a lamb. But you know what else Charlie Bat said? He said that black sheeps express everyone else's anger and pain. It's not that they have all the anger and pain— they're just the only ones who let it out. Then the other people don't have to. But you face things, Witch Baby. And you help us face things. We can learn from you. I can't stand when someone I love is sad, so I try to take it away without just letting it be. I get so caught up in being good and sweet and taking care of everyone that sometimes I don't admit when people are really in pain." Weetzie took off her pink sunglasses. "But I think you can help me learn to not be afraid, my black lamb baby witch."

When they went back into the cottage everyone was waiting to celebrate Witch Baby's return. My Secret Agent Lover Man, dressed like Charlie Chaplin, was riding his unicycle around the house. Dirk was preparing his famous homemade Weetzie pizza with sun-dried tomatoes, fresh basil, red onions,

artichoke hearts and a spinach crust. Darlene Drake,
who had arrived the day before, was helping Duck
twist balloons into slinkster dogs. Valentine and Ping
Chong presented Witch Baby with film for her camera.
Brandy-Lynn lifted her up onto Coyote's shoulders.

"I think I saw five little Joshua tree sprouts coming up across the street," Coyote said, parading with
Cherokee, Raphael, Slinkster Dog, Go-Go Girl and
the puppies following him.

Then Coyote put Witch Baby down and knelt in
front of her, like a sunrise, warming her face. "I'm
sorry about the seeds. Even if they never came up, I
shouldn't have been angry with you. We are very
much the same, Witch Baby."

Everyone else gathered around.

"We want to thank you," My Secret Agent Lover
Man said. "I've been remembering that night when
the article and the globe lamp appeared, and I realized that they must have been from you." He
scratched his chin. "I don't know how I didn't see that
before. They are beautiful gifts, the best gifts anyone
has ever given me. Gifts from my daughter."

"And I want to thank you, too," Darlene Drake

said shyly, placing a slinkster dog balloon at Witch Baby's feet. "You knew more about love than I knew. You helped me get my son back again."

"Without you, Miss Pancake Dancer Stowawitch, we might never have really known each other," said Duck, stooping to kiss Witch Baby's hand.

"Welcome home, Witch," Cherokee said. "I don't even mind my haircut anymore. I deserve it, I guess, since I did the same thing to you once. And besides, I look more like Weetzie now!"

Witch Baby snarled just a little.

"And thank you for helping me and Raphael find each other," Cherokee went on. "While you were away, Raphael told me it was your drumming I heard that day. You are the most slinkster-cool jamming drummer girl ever, and we hope you will play for us again even though we are clutch pigs sometimes."

"Yes, play!" everyone said.

My Secret Agent Lover Man set up the drums.

"I had them fixed for you," he said. "My daughter, a drummer. I knew it!"

So Witch Baby played. Tossing her head, sucking in her cheeks and popping up with the impact of each beat. Thrusting her whole body into the music and thrusting the music into the air around her. She imagined that her drums were planets and the music was all the voices of growth and light and life joined together and traveling into the universe. She imagined that she was playing for Angel Juan, turning the pain of being without him into music he could hear, distilling the flowers of pain into a perfume that he could keep with him forever.

Everyone sat in the candlelight, watching and listening and imagining they smelled salty roses in the air. Some of their mouths fell open, some of their eyes filled with tears, some of them bounced to the beat until they couldn't stand it anymore and had to get up and dance. Weetzie put her palms over her heart.

When Witch Baby was finished, everyone applauded. Weetzie kissed her face.

"And now it is time for a picture," Weetzie announced.

Witch Baby started to get her camera, but someone had set it up already.

"Come here, Baby," My Secret Agent Lover Man said. "You are as good a photographer as a drummer, but you aren't taking this one. This picture is of all of us."

He put her on his lap and they all gathered around. Weetzie set the timer on the camera and then hurried back to the group.

The picture was of all of them, as My Secret Agent Lover Man had said—himself and Weetzie, Dirk and Duck and Darlene, Valentine and Ping, Brandy-Lynn and Coyote, Cherokee and Raphael and Witch Baby.

"Twelve of us," said Weetzie. "So the twelve on the clock won't be empty anymore."

"Once upon time," Witch Baby said.

At dinner that night, Witch Baby looked up at the globe lamp in the center of the table. Suddenly, as if a genie had touched it, the lamp bloomed with jungles and forests, fields and gardens, became shining and restless with oceans and rivers, burned with fires, volcanoes and radiation, sparkled with deserts, beaches and cities, danced with bodies at work in factories and on farms, bodies in worship, playing music, loving, dying in the streets, flesh of many colors on infinite varieties of the same form of bones. And there—so tiny—Witch Baby saw their city.

This is the time we're upon.

Witch Baby looked around the table. She could see everyone's sadness. Her father was thinking about the movie he was making—the village where everyone is poisoned by something they love and worship. Witch Baby knew he was haunted with thoughts about the future of the planet. Dirk and Duck prayed that a cure would be found for the disease whose name they could not speak. Brandy-Lynn had never gotten over the death of Weetzie's father, Charlie Bat, and Darlene was with Chuck because she could not face another loss like the loss of Eddie Drake. Coyote mourned for the sky and sea, animals and vegetables, that were full of toxins. Some people hated to see Ping and Valentine together, because they weren't the same color, and Cherokee and Raphael might have to face the same hatred. Cherokee would never know for sure who her real dad was. There was Weetzie with her bitten fingernails, taking care of all these people, showing them the world she saw through pink lenses. Somewhere in Mexico, separated from Witch Baby by walls and barbed wire, floodlights and blocked-off trenches, was the Perez family—Marquez, Gabriela,

Angel Miguel, Angel Pedro, Angelina and Serafina, and Angel Juan—Angel Juan who would always be with Witch Baby, a velvet wing shadow guarding her dreams. And there was Vixanne trying to deny the grief she saw, trying to keep it from entering her body through eyes that were just like Witch Baby's eyes.

Witch Baby saw that her own sadness was only a small piece of the puzzle of pain that made up the globe. But she was a part of the globe—she had her place. And there was a lot of happiness as well, a lot of love—so much that maybe, from somewhere, far away in the universe, the cottage shone like someone's globe lamp, Witch Baby Secret Agent Black Lamb Wigg Bat thought.

cherokee bat
and the
goat guys

WIND SONG

The black Snake Wind came to me;
The Black Snake Wind came to me,
Came and wrapped itself about
Came here running with its songs.

Pima Indian

Dear Everybody,

We miss you. Witch Baby is burying herself in mud again. But don't worry. Coyote is taking care of us the way you said he would. He is going to help me make Witch Baby some wings. Coyote is teaching me all about Indians. I am a deer, Witch Baby is a raven and Raphael is a dreaming obsidian elk. I hope the film is going well. We love you.

Cherokee Thunderbat

Wings

Cherokee Bat loved the canyons. Beachwood Canyon, lined with palm trees, hibiscus, bougainvillea and a row of candles lit for the two old ladies who had been killed by a hit-and-run, led to the Hollywood sign or to the lake that changed colors under a bridge of stone bears. Topanga Canyon wound like a river to the sea past flower children, paintings of Indian goddesses and a restaurant where the tablecloths glowed purple-twilight and coyotes watched from among the leaves. Laurel Canyon had the ruins of Houdini's magic mansion, the country store where rock stars like Jim Morrison probably used to buy their beer, stained-glass Marilyn Monroes shining in the trees, leopard-spotted cars, gardens full of pink poison oleander and the Mediterranean

villa on the hill where Joni Mitchell once lived,
dreaming about clouds and carousels and guarded by
stone lions. It also had the house built of cherry wood
and antique windows where Cherokee lived with her
family.

Cherokee always felt closer to animals in the
canyons. Not just the stone lions and bears but the
real animals—silver squirrels at the lake, deer, a
flock of parrots that must have escaped their cages to
find each other, peacocks screaming in gardens and
the horses at Sunset Stables. Cherokee dreamed she
was a horse with a mane the color of a smog-sunset,
and she dreamed she was a bird with feathers like
rainbows in oil puddles. She would wake up and go to
the mirror. She wanted to be faster, quieter, darker,
shimmering. So she ran around the lake, up the trails,
along winding canyon roads, trying not to make noise,
barefoot so her feet would get tougher or in beaded
moccasins when they hurt too much. Then she went
back to the mirror. She was too naked. She wanted
hooves, haunches, a beak, claws, wings.

There was a collage of dead butterflies on the wall
of the canyon house where Cherokee lived with her

almost-sister Witch Baby and the rest of their family. At night Cherokee dreamed the butterflies came to life, broke the glass and flew out at her in a storm, covering her with silky pollen. When she woke up she painted her dream. She searched for feathers everywhere—collected them in canyons and on beaches, comparing the shapes and colors, sketching them, trying to understand how they worked. Then she studied pictures of birds and pasted the feathers down in wing patterns. But it wasn't until Witch Baby began to bury herself that Cherokee decided to make the wings.

Witch Baby was Cherokee's almost-sister but they were very different. Cherokee's white-blonde hair was as easy to comb as water and she kept it in many long braids; Witch Baby's dark hair was a seaweed clump of tangles. It formed little angry balls that Witch Baby tugged at with her fingers until they pulled right out. Cherokee, who ran and danced, had perfect posture. Witch Baby's shoulders hunched up to her ears from years of creeping around taking candid photographs and from playing her drums. Cherokee wore white suede moccasins and turquoise and silver beads; Witch Baby's toes curled like snails inside her cowboy-boot roller-skates and she wore an assortment of whatever she could find until she decided she would rather wear mud.

One day, Witch Baby went into the backyard, took off all her clothes and began to roll around in the wet earth. She smeared mud everywhere, clumped handfuls into her hair, stuffed it in her ears, up her nostrils and even ate some. She slid around on her belly through the mud. Then she slid into the garden shed and lay there in the dark without moving.

Cherokee and Witch Baby's family, Weetzie Bat and My Secret Agent Lover Man, Brandy-Lynn Bat and Dirk and Duck, were away in South America shooting a movie about magic. They had left Cherokee and Witch Baby under the care of their friend Coyote, but Cherokee hated to bother him. He lived on top of a hill and was always very busy with his chants and dances and meditative rituals. So Cherokee decided to try to take care of Witch Baby by herself. She went into the shed and said, "Witch Baby, come out. We'll go to Farmer's Market and get date shakes and look at the puppies in the pet store

there and figure out a way to rescue them." But Witch
Baby buried herself deeper in the mud.

"Witch Baby, come out and play drums for me,"
Cherokee said. "You are the most slinkster-jamming
drummer girl and I want to dance." But Witch Baby
shut her eyes and swallowed a handful of gritty dirt.

Cherokee heard Witch Baby's thoughts in her own
head.

*I am a seed in the slippery, silent, blind, breathless
dark. I have no nose or mouth, ears or eyes to see. Just
a skin of satin black and a secret green dream deep
inside.*

For hours, Cherokee begged Witch Baby to come
out. Finally she went into the house and called the boy
who had been her best friend for as long as she could
remember—Raphael Chong Jah-Love.

Raphael was practicing his guitar at the house
down the street where he lived with his parents,
Valentine and Ping Chong Jah-Love. Valentine and
Ping were away in South America with Cherokee and
Witch Baby's family working on the movie.

"Witch Baby is buried in mud!" Cherokee told
Raphael when he answered the phone. "She won't

come out of the shed. Could you ask her to play drums with us?"

"Witch Baby is the best drummer I know, Kee," Raphael said. "But she'll never play drums with us."

Raphael and Cherokee wanted to start a band but they needed a bass player and a drummer. Witch Baby had always refused to help them.

"Just ask her to play for you then, just once," Cherokee begged. "I am really worried about her."

So Raphael tossed his dreadlocks, put on his John Lennon sunglasses, and rode his bicycle through sunlight and wind chimes and bird shadows to Cherokee's house.

He found Cherokee in the backyard among the fruit trees and roses knocking at the door of the shed. Witch Baby had locked herself in.

"Come out, Witch Baby," said Raphael. "I need to hear your drumming for inspiration. Even if you won't be in our band."

Cherokee kissed his powdered-chocolate-colored cheek. There was still no sound from inside the shed.

Cherokee and Raphael stood outside the shed for

a long time. It got dark and stars came out, shining on the damp lawn.

"Let's go eat something," Raphael said. "Witch Baby will smell the food and come out."

They went inside and Cherokee took one of the frozen homemade pizzas that Weetzie had left them when the family went away, and put it in the oven. Raphael played an Elvis Presley record, lit some candles and made a salad. Cherokee opened all the windows—the stained-glass roses, the leaded glass arches, the one that looked like rain—so Witch Baby would smell the melting cheese, hear it sizzle along with "Hound Dog" and come out of the mud shed. But when they had finished their pizza, there was still no sign of Witch Baby. They left two big slices of pizza in front of the shed. Then they set up Cherokee's tepee on the lawn, curled into their sleeping bags and told ghost stories until they fell asleep.

In the morning, the pizza looked as if it had been nibbled on by a mouse. Cherokee hoped the mouse had tangled hair, purple tilty eyes and curly toes, but the door of the shed was still locked.

Witch Baby would not come out of the mud shed. Cherokee finally decided she would have to ask Coyote what to do. With his wisdom and grace, he was the only one who would know how to bring Witch Baby out of the mud.

Early that morning, Cherokee took a bus into the hills where Coyote lived. She got off the bus and walked up the steep, winding streets to his shack. He was among the cactus plants doing his daily stretching, breathing and strengthening exercises when she found him. Below him the city was waking up under a layer of smog. Coyote turned his head slowly toward Cherokee and opened his eyes. Cherokee held her breath.

"Cherokee Bat," said Coyote in a voice that reminded her of sun-baked red rock, "are you all right? Why have you come?"

"Witch Baby is burying herself in mud," Cherokee told him. "She won't come out of the shed. We keep trying to help her but nothing works. I didn't know what else to do."

Coyote walked to the edge of the cactus garden and looked down at the layer of smog hovering over the city. He sighed and raised his deeply lined palms to the sky.

"No wonder Witch Baby is burying herself in mud," he said, looking out at the city drowning in smog. "There is dirt everywhere, real filth. We should not be able to see air. Air should be like the lenses of our eyes. And the sea . . . we should be able to swim in the sea; the sea should be like our tears and our sweat—clear and natural for us. There should be animals all around us—not hiding in the poison darkness, watching with their yellow eyes. Look at this city. Look what we have done."

Cherokee looked at the city and then she looked down at her hands. She felt small and pale and naked.

Coyote turned to Cherokee and put his hand on her shoulder. The early sun had filled the lines of his palm and now Cherokee felt it burning into her shoulder blade.

"The earth Witch Baby is burying herself in is purer than what surrounds us," Coyote said. "Maybe she feels it will protect her. Maybe she is growing up in it like a plant."

"But Coyote," Cherokee said. "She can't stay

there forever in the mud shed. She hardly moves or eats anything."

Coyote looked back out at the city. Then he turned to Cherokee again and said softly, "I will help you to help Witch Baby. You must make her some wings."

A strong wind came. It dried the leaves to paper and the paper to flames like paint. Then it sent the flames through the papery hills and canyons, painting them red. It knocked over telephone poles and young trees and sent trash cans crashing in the streets. The wind made Cherokee's hair crackle with blue electric sparks. It made a kind of lemonade—cracking the glass chimes that hung in the lemon tree outside Cherokee's window into ice and tossing the lemons to the ground so they split open. It brought Cherokee the sea and the burning hills and faraway gardens. It brought her the days and nights early; she smelled the smoky dawn in the darkness, the damp dark while it was still light. And, finally, the wind brought her feathers.

She was standing with Coyote among the cactus and they were chanting to the animals hidden in the world below them, "You are all my relations." It was dawn and the wind was wild. Cherokee tried to understand what it was saying. There was a halo of blue sparks around her head.

"Wind, bring us the feathers that birds no longer need," Coyote chanted. "Hawk and dove. Tarred feathers of the gull. Shimmer peacock plumes. Jewel green of parrots and other kept birds. Witch Baby needs help leaving the mud."

The wind sounded wilder. Cherokee looked out at the horizon. As the sun rose, the sky filled with feathery pink clouds. Then it seemed as if the clouds were flying toward Cherokee and Coyote. The rising sun flashed in their eyes for a moment, and as Cherokee stood, blind on the hilltop, she felt softness on her skin. The wind was full of feathers.

Small, bright feathers like petals, plain gray ones, feathers flecked with gleaming iridescent lights like tiny tropical waves. They swirled around Cherokee and Coyote, tickling their faces. Cherokee felt as if she could lift her arms and be carried away on wings of feathers and wind. She imagined flying over the city looking down at the tiny cars, palm trees, pools and lawns—all of it so ordered and calm—and not having to worry about anything. She imagined what her house would look like from above with its stained-glass skylights and rooftop deck, the garden with its fruit trees, roses, hot tub and wooden shed. And then she remembered Witch Baby slithering around in the mud. That was what this was all about—wings for Witch Baby.

The wind died down and the feathers settled around Cherokee and Coyote. They gathered the feathers, filling a big basket Coyote had brought from his shack.

"Now you can make the wings," Coyote said.

Cherokee looked at her hands.

Cherokee took wires and bent them into wing-shaped frames. Then she covered the frames with thin, stiff gauze, and over that she pasted the feathers the wind had brought. It took her a long time. She worked every day after school until late into the night. She hardly ate, did her homework or slept. At school she finally fell asleep on her desk and dreamed of falling into a feather bed. The dream-bed tore and feathers got into her nostrils and throat. She woke up coughing and the teacher sent her out of the room.

"What is wrong, Cherokee?" Raphael asked her on the phone when she wouldn't come over to play music with him. "You are acting as crazy as your sister."

But she only sighed and pasted down another feather in its place. "I can't tell you yet. Don't worry. You'll find out on Witch Baby's birthday."

The rain was like a green forest descending over the city. Cherokee danced in puddles and caught raindrops off flower petals with her tongue. Her lungs didn't fill with smog when she ran. She loved the rain but she was worried, too. She was worried about Witch Baby getting sick out in the shed.

Cherokee brought blankets and a thermos of hot soup and put them outside the door. Witch Baby took the blankets and soup when no one was looking, but she didn't let Cherokee inside the shed.

When Witch Baby's birthday came, Cherokee and Raphael planned a big party for her. They made three kinds of salsa and a special dish of crumbled corn bread, green chiles, artichoke hearts, cheese and red peppers. They bought chips and soda and an ice-cream cake and decorated the house with tiny blinking colored lights, piñatas, big red balloons and black rubber bats. All their friends came, bringing incense, musical instruments, candles and flowers. Everyone ate, drank and danced to a tape Raphael had made of African music, salsa, zydeco, blues and soul. It was a perfect party except for one thing. Witch Baby wasn't there. She was still hiding in the shed.

Finally, Raphael got his guitar and began to play and sing some of Witch Baby's favorite songs—"Black Magic Woman," "Lust for Life," "Leader of the Pack" and "Wild Thing." Cherokee sang, too, and played her tambourine. Suddenly, the door opened and a boy came in. He was carrying a bass guitar and was dressed in baggy black pants, a white shirt buttoned to the collar and thick black shoes. A bandana was tied over his black hair. Everyone stopped and stared at him. Cherokee rubbed her eyes. It was Angel Juan Perez.

When Witch Baby was very little, she had fallen in love with Angel Juan, but he had had to go back to Mexico with his family. He still wrote to Witch Baby on her birthday and holidays and she said she dreamed about him all the time.

"Angel Juan!" Cherokee cried. She and Raphael ran to him and they all embraced.

"Where've you been?" Raphael asked.

"Mexico," said Angel Juan. "I've been playing music there since my family and I were sent back. I knew someday I'd get to see you guys again. And how is . . .?"

"Witch Baby isn't so great," said Cherokee. "She won't come out of the shed in back."

"What?" said Angel Juan. "Niña Bruja! My sweet, wild, purple-eyes!"

"Come and play some music for her," said Raphael. "Maybe she'll hear you and come out."

Witch Baby, huddling in the mud shed, smelled the food and saw colored lights blinking through the window. She even imagined the ice cream cake glistening in the freezer. But nothing was enough to make her leave the shed until she heard a boy's voice singing a song.

"Niña Bruja," sang the voice.

Witch Baby stood up in the dark shed, shivering.

129

Mud was caked all over her body, making her look like a strange animal with glowing purple eyes. It was raining when she stepped outside, and the water rinsed off the mud, leaving her naked and even colder. The voice drew her to the window of the house and she stared in.

Cherokee was the only one who noticed Witch Baby clinging to the windowsill and watching Angel Juan through the rain-streaked stained-glass irises. Cherokee ran and got a purple silk kimono robe embroidered with dragons, went out into the rain, slipped the robe on Witch Baby's hungry body, pried her fingers from the windowsill and took her hand. Hiding behind her tangled hair, Witch Baby followed Cherokee into the house as if she were in a trance.

Cherokee handed Witch Baby a pair of drumsticks and helped her tiptoe past everyone to the drums they had set up for her behind Raphael and Angel Juan. Witch Baby sat at her drums for a moment, biting her lip and staring at the back of Angel Juan's head. Then she lunged forward with her body and began to play.

Everyone turned to see what was happening. The

drumming was powerful. It was almost impossible to believe it was coming through the body of a half-starved young girl who had been hiding in the mud for weeks. As Witch Baby played, a pair of multicolored wings descended from the ceiling. They shimmered in the lights as if they were in flight, reflecting the dawns and cities and sunsets they passed, then rested gently near Witch Baby's shoulders. Cherokee attached them there. The wings looked as if they had always been a part of Witch Baby's body, and the music she played made them tremble. Angel Juan turned to stare. Once everyone had caught their breath, they tossed their heads, st   d their feet, shook their hips, and began to dance. Cherokee got her tambourine and joined the band.

When the song was over, Cherokee brought out the ice-cream cake burning with candles and everyone sang "Happy Birthday, dear Witch Baby." It was hard for Cherokee to recognize her almost-sister. Glowing from music, and magical in the Cherokee wind-wings, Witch Baby was beautiful. Angel Juan could not take his eyes off her.

After she had blown out all the candles, he came

up and took her hand. "Niña Bruja," he said, "I've missed you so much."

Witch Baby looked up at Angel Juan's smooth, brown face with the high cheekbones, the black-spark eyes. The last time she had seen him, he was a tiny blur of a boy.

"Dance with me," he said.

Witch Baby looked down at her bare, curly toes. There was still mud under her toenails, but the wings made her feel safe.

"Dance with me, Niña Bruja," Angel Juan said again. He put his hands on Witch Baby's shoulders, hunched tightly beneath the wings, and she relaxed. Then he took one of her hands, uncurling the fingers, and began to dance with her in the protective shade of many feathers. Witch Baby pressed her head of wild hair against Angel Juan's clean, white shirt.

Everyone clapped for them, then found partners and joined in. Cherokee stood watching. She remembered how Witch Baby and Angel Juan had played together when they were very young, how Witch Baby had covered her walls with pictures she had taken of him, how she never bit her nails or pulled at her snarl-balls or hissed or spit when he was around. Then he had had to leave so suddenly when his family was sent back to Mexico.

Now, seeing them dancing together, the nape of Angel Juan's neck exposed as he bent to hold Witch Baby, the black flames of her hair pressed against his chest, Cherokee felt like crying.

Raphael came up to Cherokee and took her hands. For almost their whole lives, Cherokee and Raphael had been inseparable, but tonight Cherokee felt something new. It was something tight and slidey in her stomach, something burning and shivery in her spine; it was like having hearts beating in her throat and knees. Raphael had never looked so much like a lion with his black eyes and mane of dreadlocks.

"The wings are beautiful, Kee," Raphael said. "They are the best gift anyone could give to Witch Baby." He lifted Cherokee's hands into the light and examined them. "How did you do it?" he asked.

"Love."

"You are magic," Raphael said. "I've known that since we were babies, but now your magic is very strong. I think you are going to have to be careful."

"Careful?" said Cherokee. "What do you mean?"

"Never mind," said Raphael. "I just got a funny feeling. I just want things to stay like this forever." And he stroked Cherokee's long, yellow braids, but he didn't put his arms around her the way he had always done before.

SONG OF ENCOURAGEMENT

Within my bowl there lies
Shining dizziness,
Bubbling drunkenness.

There are great whirlwinds
Standing upside down above us.
They lie within my bowl.

A great bear heart,
A great eagle heart,
A great hawk heart,
A great twisting wind—
All these have gathered here
And lie within my bowl.

Now you will drink it.

Papago Indian

Dear Everybody,

Witch Baby is fine! Angel Juan came back. He got here on Witch Baby's birthday! That was her best present but I also gave her some wings Coyote helped me make. She looks like she will fly away. Angel Juan moved in with Raphael and Witch Baby is still sleeping in the garden shed but she isn't doing the mud thing anymore. We started a band called The Goat Guys. We are going to play out soon, I think. Raphael is the most slinkster-cool singer and guitar player. We all send our love.

Cherokee

Haunches

After Witch Baby's birthday, Cherokee, Raphael, Witch Baby and Angel Juan decided to form a band called The Goat Guys. Every day, when Angel Juan got home from the restaurant where he worked and the others from school, they practiced in Raphael's garage with posters of Bob Marley, The Beatles, The Doors and John Lennon and a velvet painting of Elvis on the walls around them. Witch Baby sat at her drums, her purple eyes fierce, her skinny arms pounding out the beat; Angel Juan pouted and swayed as he played his bass, and Raphael sang in a voice like Kahlúa and milk, swinging his dreadlocks to the sound of his guitar. Cherokee, whirling with her tambourine, imagined she could see their music like fireworks—flashing flowers and fountains of light exploding in the air around them.

One night, Cherokee and Raphael were walking through the streets of Hollywood. Because it had just rained and was almost Christmas, a twinkling haze covered the whole city.

They passed stucco bungalows with Christmas trees shining in the windows and roses in the courtyard gardens. They stopped to catch raindrops off the rose petals with their tongues.

"What does this smell like?" Cherokee asked, sniffing a yellow rose.

"Lemonade."

"And the orange ones smell like peaches."

Raphael put his face inside a white rose. "Rain," he said.

They walked on Melrose with its neon, lovers, frozen yogurt and Italian restaurants, Santa Monica with its thin boys on bus-stop benches, lonely hot dog stands, auto repair shops where the cars glowed with fluorescent raindrops, Sunset with its billboard mouths calling you toward the sea, and Hollywood where golden lights arched from movie palace to movie palace over fake snow, pavement stars, ghetto blasters, drug dealers, pinball players and women in high-heeled pumps walking in Marilyn's footprints in front of the Chinese Theater.

Cherokee and Raphael made shadow animals with their hands when they came to bare walls. They stopped for ice-cream cones. Cherokee heard Raphael's voice singing in her head as she sucked a marshmallow out of her scoop of rocky road.

"We are ready to play out," she told him. They were hopping from star to star on Hollywood Boulevard.

"I don't know. I'm not sure I want to deal with the whole nightclub scene," he said.

"But it would be good for people to hear you." She looked at him. Raindrops had fallen off some of the roses they had been smelling and sparkled in his dreadlocks. He was wearing a denim jacket and jeans and he stepped lightly on his toes as if he weren't quite touching the ground.

He shrugged. "I don't think it's so important. I like to just play for our friends."

"But other people need our music, too. Let's just

send the tape around," Cherokee said. She looked up and pointed to the spotlights fanning across the cloudy sky. "I think you are a star, Raphael. You're my star. I'll send the tapes for us."

He shook his head so his hair flew out, scattering the drops of rain. "Okay, okay. You can if you really want to."

Let's not be afraid, Cherokee thought. Let's not be afraid of anything that can't really hurt us. She grabbed his wrist and they ran across the street as the red stoplight hand flashed.

Cherokee sent Goat Guy tapes to nightclubs around the city. She put a photograph that Witch Baby had taken of the band on the front of the cassette. Zombo of Zombo's Rockin' Coffin called her and said he could book a show just before Christmas.

When Cherokee told Raphael, he got very quiet. "I'm not sure we're ready," he said, but she kissed him and told him they were a rockin' slink-chunk, slam-dunk band and that it would be fine.

On the night of the first show, Raphael lit a cigarette.

"What are you doing?" Cherokee said, trying to

grab it out of his hand. They were sitting backstage at the Coffin. Raphael coughed but then he took another hit.

"Leave me alone." He got up and paced back and forth.

Angel Juan and Witch Baby came with Witch Baby's drums.

"What's wrong, man?" Angel Juan asked, but Raphael just took another puff of smoke.

Cherokee had never seen him look like this. There were dark circles under his eyes and his skin seemed faded. And he had never told her to leave him alone before.

Cherokee kissed Raphael's cheek and went to the front of the club. It was decorated with pieces of black fabric, sickly-looking Cupids, candles and fake, greenish lilies. The people seated at the tables had the same coloring as the flowers. They were slumped over their drinks waiting for the music to begin.

Cherokee turned to see a short, fat man in a tuxedo staring at her. His chubby fingers with their longish nails were wrapped around a tall glass of steaming blue liquid.

"Aren't you a little young to be in my club?"

"I'm in the band," Cherokee said.

"You sure don't look like a Goat Guy." He eyed her up and down and wiped his mouth with the back of his hand.

Cherokee glared at him.

"Sorry to stare. I always stare at how girls do their makeup. It's a business thing. I like that blue line around your eyes."

She started to edge away.

"I used to be an undertaker before I opened this place. Still got family in the business. Maybe you could come with me sometime and make up a few faces. You did your eyes real nice."

Cherokee could smell Zombo's breath. Her stomach churned and tumbled. "I better go get ready," she said, feeling him watching as she walked backstage.

When the band came on, Cherokee saw Zombo leering up at her with his hands in his pants pockets. She saw the rest of the hollow-eyed audience lurched forward on their elbows and guzzling their drinks. Standing there in the spotlight, she felt an icy wave crash in her chest and she knew that she was not going to be able to play or sing or dance. She could tell that the rest of The Goat Guys were frozen too. Witch Baby lost a drumstick right away and started to jump up and down, gnashing her teeth. When Angel Juan played the wrong chords, he frowned and rolled his eyes. But it was Raphael who suffered more than anyone that night. He stood trembling on the stage with his dreadlocks hanging in his face. His voice strained from his throat so that Cherokee could hardly recognize it.

The Coffin crowd began to hiss and spit. Some threw cigarette butts and maraschino cherries at the stage. When a cherry hit Raphael in the temple, he looked helplessly around him, then turned and disappeared behind the black curtain. Witch Baby thrust her middle finger into the air and waved it around.

"Clutch pigs!" she shouted.

Then, she, Cherokee and Angel Juan followed Raphael backstage, ducking to miss the objects flying through the air at them.

Raphael hardly spoke to anyone after Zombo's Coffin. He didn't want to rehearse or play basketball,

surf or talk or eat. He lay in his room under the hieroglyphics he and Cherokee had once painted on his
wall, listened to Jimi Hendrix, Led Zeppelin and The
Doors and smoked more and more cigarettes.
Cherokee came over with chocolates and oranges
and strands of beads she had strung, but he only
glared at her and turned up the volume on his stereo.
She didn't know what to say.

When Christmas came, Cherokee, Witch Baby
and Angel Juan planned a party to cheer Raphael up
and keep them all from missing their families. Angel
Juan drove his red pickup truck downtown at dawn to
a place by the railroad tracks and came back with a
pink snow-sugared tree that Witch Baby and
Cherokee decorated with feathers, beads, and miniature globes; Kachina, Barbie, and Japanese baby
dolls; and Mexican skeletons. They filled the rooms
with pine branches, red berries, pink poinsettias, tiny
white lights, strands of colored stars and salsa and
gospel music. They baked cookies in the shapes of
hieroglyphics and Indian symbols and breads in the
shapes of angels and mermaids.

On Christmas Eve they made hot cinnamon cider,

corn bread, yams, salad and cranberry salmon and invited Raphael over. The table was an island of candles and flowers and cascading mountains of food floating in the dark sea of the room.

And we are the stars in the sky, Cherokee thought, seeing all their faces circling the table.

Raphael was hunched in his chair playing with his food. She had never seen him look so far away from her.

After dinner they opened presents in front of the fire. Big packages had arrived from their families—leather backpacks, woven blankets, painted saints and angels, mysterious stones, beaded scarves and candelabra in the shapes of pink mermaids and blue doves. Coyote, who had been invited but did not want to leave his hilltop, had painted Indian birth charts for everyone—Cherokee the deer, Witch Baby the raven, Raphael and Angel Juan the elks. Everyone loved their presents except for Raphael. He didn't seem to care about anything.

"Raphael," Cherokee whispered, "what do you want me to give you for Christmas?"

The fire crackled and embers showered down.

The air smelled of pine and cinnamon.

Raphael just stared at her body without saying anything, his eyes reflecting the flames, and Cherokee was glad she was wrapped in one of the woven blankets her family had sent.

The next day Cherokee went to see Coyote. He was watering the vegetables he grew among his cactus plants.

"Our first show was terrible," she told him.

"Yes?"

"Raphael is very upset. I don't know what to do."

"You must practice."

"He won't even pick up his guitar."

"What did you come to me for, Cherokee?"

"I was wondering," she said, "if maybe you would help me make something for Raphael. The wings helped Witch Baby so much."

Coyote squinted at the sun. "And what do you think would help Raphael?"

"Not wings. Maybe some goat pants would help. Then he'd feel like a Goat Guy and not be so scared on stage. He's really good, Coyote. He just gets stage fright."

Coyote sighed and shook his head.

"Please, Coyote. Just one more gift. I am really worried that Raphael will hurt himself. It's kind of hard for him with his parents away and everything."

Coyote sighed again. "I did promise all your parents I would help you," he said. "But I must think about this. Go now. I must think alone."

So Cherokee went to Raphael's house, where she found him lying on his bed in the dark listening to Jimi Hendrix and smoking a cigarette. She sat cross-legged beside him. The moonlight fell across the blankets in tiger stripes.

"What?" he growled.

"Nothing. I just came to be with you."

Raphael turned his back, and when she tried to stroke his shoulder through the thin T-shirt, he jerked away.

"Come on, Raphael, let's play some music."

"I am playing music," he said, turning up the volume on the stereo.

"We can't just give up."

"I can."

Cherokee wanted to touch him. She felt the tingling

sliding from her scalp down her spine and back again. "We need practice, that's all. That club wasn't the right place anyway." As she spoke, she loosened her braids, tossing her gold hair near his face like a cloud of flowers.

He stirred a little, awakened by her, then smashed his cigarette into an Elvis ashtray. She noticed how thick the veins were in his arms, the strain in his throat, the width of his knees in his jeans. He seemed older, suddenly. The small brown body she had grown up with, sprawled beside on warm rocks, painted pictures on, slept beside in her tepee, was no longer so familiar. He reached out and barely stroked the blonde bouquet of her hair with the back of his hand. Then, suddenly, he grabbed her wrists and pulled her toward him. Cherokee didn't recognize the flat, dark look in Raphael's eyes. She pulled away, twisting her wrists so they slipped from his hands.

"I have to go," she said.

"Cherokee!" His voice sounded hoarse.

"I'll talk to you tomorrow." Cherokee backed out of the room. When she got outside she heard howling and the trees looked like shadow cats ready to spring.

She thought there were men hiding in the dark, watching her run down the street in her thin, white moccasins.

The next day, after school, Cherokee went to see Coyote again. He was standing in his cactus garden as if waiting for her, but when she went to greet him he didn't say anything. He turned away, shut his eyes and began to hum and chant. The sounds hissed like fire, became deep water, then blended together, as hushed as smoke. Cherokee felt the sounds in her own chest—imagined flames and rivers and clouds filling her so that she wanted to dance them. But she stayed very still and listened.

Cherokee and Coyote stood on the hillside for a long time. Cherokee tried not to be impatient, but an hour passed, then another, and even Coyote's chants were not mesmerizing enough to make her forget that she had to find a way to make goat pants or something for Raphael. It was getting dark.

Coyote turned his broad face up to the sky and kept chanting. It seemed as if the darkening sky were touching him, Cherokee thought, pressing lightly against his eyelids and palms, as if the leaves in the trees were shivering to be near him, even the pebbles on the hillside shifting, and then she saw that pebbles were moving, sliding down; the leaves were shaking and singing in harsh, throaty voices. Or something was singing. Something was coming.

The goats clambered down sideways toward Cherokee and Coyote. A whirlwind of dust and fur. Their jaws and beards swung from side to side; their eyes blinked.

"I guess these are the real goat guys," Cherokee said.

Coyote opened his eyes and the goats gathered around his legs. He laid his palms on each of their skulls, one at a time, in the bony hollow between the horns. They were all suddenly very quiet.

Coyote turned and the goats followed him into his shack, butting each other as they went. Cherokee stood in the doorway and watched as Coyote lit candles and sheared the thick, shaggy fur off the goat haunches. They did not complain. When he was done with one, the next would come, not even flinching at the buzz of the electric shears. The dusty fur piled up on the floor of the shack, and when the last and smallest goat had been shorn, they all scrambled away out the door, up the hillside and into the night.

Cherokee watched their naked backsides disappearing into the brush. She wanted to thank them but she didn't know what to say. How do you thank a bare-bottomed goat who is rushing up a mountain after he has just given you his fur? she wondered.

Coyote stood in the dim shack. Cherokee noticed that his hair was even shinier with perspiration. She had never seen him sweat before. He frowned at the pile of fur.

"Well, Cherokee Bat," Coyote said, "here is your fur. Use it well. The fur and the feathers were gifts that the animals gave you without death, untainted. But think of the animals that have died for their hides, and for their beauty and power. Think of them, too, when you sew for your friends."

Cherokee gathered the fur in bags and thanked Coyote. She wanted to leave right away without even asking him how to go about making the haunches. There was a mute, remote look on his face as if he were trying to remember something.

When Cherokee got home, she thought of Coyote's

expression and blinked to send the image away. It frightened her. She washed the fur, pulling out nettles and leaves, watching the dark water swirl down the drain. The next day she dried the fur in the sun. But she did not know what to do next.

For nights she lay awake, trying to decide how to make haunches. She dreamed of goats dancing in misty forest glades, rising on their hind legs as they danced, wreathed with flowers, baring their teeth, drunk on flower pollen, staggering, leaping. She dreamed of girls too—pale and naked, being chased by the goats. The girls tried to cover their nakedness but the heavy, hairy goat heads swung toward them, teeth chewing flowers, eyes menacing, the forest closing in around, leaves chiming like bells.

Cherokee woke up clutching the sheets around her body. The room smelled of goat, and she got up to open the windows. As she leaned out into the night, filling herself with the fragrance of the canyon, she thought of Raphael's heavy dreadlocks, the cords of hair like fur. She had spent hours winding beads and feathers into his hair and her own. Now she loosened her braids.

She knew, suddenly, how she would make the pants.

Cherokee braided and braided strands of fur together. Then she attached the braids to a pair of Raphael's old jeans. She put extra fur along the hips so the pants really looked like shaggy goat legs. She made a tail with the rest of the fur. When she was finished, Cherokee brought the haunches to Raphael's house and left them at the door in a box covered with leaves and flowers.

That night he called her: "I'm coming over," and hung up.

She went to the mirror, took off her T-shirt and looked at her naked body. Too thin, she thought, too pale. She wished she were dark like the skins of certain cherries and had bigger breasts. Quickly she dressed again, brushed her hair and touched some of Weetzie's gardenia perfume to the place at her throat where she could feel her heart.

When Raphael came to the door, Cherokee saw him through the peephole at first—silhouetted against the night with his long, ropy hair, his chest bare under his denim jacket, his fur legs.

Cherokee opened the door and he walked in heavily, strutting, not floating. The tail swung behind him as he went straight to Cherokee's room and turned off the light. She hesitated at the door.

"They look good," she said.

Raphael stared at her. "Things are different now." His voice was hoarse. "Come here."

His teeth and eyes flashed, reflecting the light from the hallway. He was like a forest creature who didn't belong inside.

Cherokee tried to breathe. She wanted to go to him and stroke his head. She wanted to paint red and silver flowers on his chest and then curl up beside him in her tepee the way she used to do. But he was right. Things were different now.

Then, without even realizing it, she was standing next to him. They were still almost the same height. She could smell him—cocoa, a light basketball sweat. She could see his lips.

All their lives, Cherokee and Raphael had given each other little kisses, but this kiss was like a wind from the desert, a wind that knocks over candles so that flowers catch fire, a wind, or like a sunset in the desert casting sphinx shadows on the sand, a sunset, or like a shivering in the spine of the earth. They collapsed, their hands sliding down each other's arms. Then they were reeling over and over among the feathers and dried flowers that covered Cherokee's floor. She remembered how they had rolled down hills together, tangling and untangling, the smell of crushed grass and coconut sun lotion and barbecue smoke all mixed up in their heads. Then, when she had rolled against him, she hardly felt it—they were like one body. Now each touch stung and sparkled. He grasped her hair in his hand and kissed her neck, then pressed his face between her breasts as if he were trying to get inside to her heart.

"White Dawn," he whispered. "Cherokee White Dawn."

Suddenly she couldn't swallow—the air thick around her like waves of dark dreadlocks—and she pushed him away.

Raphael put his hands on his stomach. He glared at her. "What are you doing?"

Cherokee ran out of the room, out of the house, to the garden shed where Witch Baby was practicing her drums. Cherokee leaned her head against the wall, feeling the pounding go through her body.

"What's wrong with you?" Witch Baby asked when she had finished playing.

"Can I stay here tonight?"

"Why? Is Raphael being a wild thing?"

"I just don't feel like being in the house," Cherokee said.

"*Sure!*" said Witch Baby. "I bet it's because of Raphael. I just hope you use birth control like Weetzie told us."

Cherokee frowned and started to turn away.

"I guess you can stay if you want," Witch Baby said.

Cherokee curled up next to Witch Baby but she didn't sleep all night. She lay awake with the moon pouring over her through the shed window, bleaching her skin even whiter. Sometimes she thought she heard Witch Baby's hoarse voice singing her a mysterious lullaby, but she wasn't sure.

After that, Cherokee was afraid to see Raphael, but he called her a few days later and said there would be a rehearsal at his house the next day. It was the first time he had suggested that they play music since Zombo's Coffin.

Raphael wore the fur pants. He didn't say much to Cherokee but he sang and played better than ever. When they were done, he said, "I booked a gig for us."

"Where at?" Angel Juan asked, peering over the top of his sunglasses.

"I thought you didn't want to play," Witch Baby said.

"It's at The Vamp. We'd be opening for The Devil Dogs."

"Sounds kind of creepy!" Cherokee said, but she was glad that Raphael wanted to play again.

"The owner, Lulu, heard our tape. She is really into us." Raphael stomped over to the mirror, puffed out his chest and modeled the fur pants. "The Goat Guys are ready for anything now."

Lulu was tall and black-cherry skinned with waves of dark hair and large breasts. She moved gracefully in her short red dress.

"How do you like the club?" Lulu asked Raphael,

brushing his arm with her fingertips.

The Vamp was dark with black skull candles burning and stuffed animal heads on the walls. Cherokee shivered.

"It's a great setup. Thanks, a lot," he said, looking at Lulu's lips as if he were in a trance.

Lulu smiled. "I think you'll be just great here, honey. Let me know if you need anything."

She walked away, shifting her hips precisely from side to side. Raphael watched her go.

"Raphael!" Cherokee said. A stuffed deer head had its glass eyes fixed on her.

"Let's do a sound check," Raphael said to his cigarette.

Maybe it was the fact that they had been rehearsing or that after the first show it just got easier, or maybe it was the goat pants. Or maybe, Cherokee thought, it was the anger Raphael felt toward her after the night in her bedroom—the power of that. Whatever the reason, Raphael was not the frightened boy who had left the Rockin' Coffin stage before the first song was over.

He strutted, he staggered, he jerked, he swirled his dreadlocks and his tail. He bared his teeth. He touched his bare chest. His sweat flew into the audience.

The audience howled, panted and crowded nearer to the stage, their faces bony as the wax skull candles they held above their heads. The flame shadows danced across Raphael's face.

With the heat pressing toward them and Raphael's bittersweet voice and reeling body moving them, Angel Juan, Witch Baby and Cherokee began to play better than they had ever played before. Cherokee felt as if the band were becoming one lashing, shimmery creature that the room full of people in leather wanted to devour. Someone reached up and pulled at her skirt, and she whirled away from the edge of the stage. The room was spinning but even as she felt hunted, trapped, about to be devoured by the crowd at the foot of the stage, she also felt free, flickering above them, able to hypnotize, powerful. The power of the trapped animal who is, for that moment, perfect, the hunter's only thought and desire.

When the set was over, the band slipped backstage away from the shrieks and the bones and the burning. Raphael turned to Cherokee, drenched and feverish. She was afraid he would turn away again but instead he took her face in his hands and kissed her cheeks.

"Thank you, Cherokee White Dawn," he murmured.

Then they were running, holding hands and running out of the club. They ran through the streets of Hollywood but Cherokee hardly noticed the fallen stars, the neon cocktail glasses. They could have been anywhere—a forest, a desert—running in the moon-shadow of the sphinx, a jungle where the night was green. They could have been goats, horses, wildcats. They could have been dreaming or running through someone else's dream.

They ran to Raphael's house. Cherokee felt a metallic pinch between her eyes, something hot and wet on her upper lip. She touched her nose and looked at her fingers. "I'm bleeding."

Raphael helped her lie down on his bed. He brought a wet cloth and pressed it against her nose. "Keep your head back."

"I get too excited, I guess."

As he cradled her head in one hand, he began kissing her throat, the insides of her elbows and wrists for a long time. Then he kissed her forehead and temples. "Is it better?"

She moved the cloth away and sat up. It was dark in the room but the animals, pyramids, eyes and lotus flowers glimmered on the moonlit wall. Cherokee and Raphael were both sweaty and tangled. She could smell his chocolate, her vanilla-gardenia, and something else that was both mingling together.

"Coyote told me about Indian women who fell in love with men because of their flute playing and got nosebleeds when they heard the music because they were so excited," Cherokee said.

"Does it work with a guitar?"

"It works when I look at you."

He touched her face. "You're okay now, I think. . . . I miss you, Cherokee. I want to wake up with you in the morning the way we used to. But different. It's different now."

It was different. It was light-filled red waves breaking on a beach again and again—a salt-stung fullness. It was being the waves and riding the waves. The bed lifted, the house and the lawn and the garden and the street and the night, one ocean rocking them, tossing them, an ocean of liquid coral roses.

Afterward, Cherokee was washed ashore with her head on his chest. She could hear the echo of herself inside of him.

SONG OF THE FALLEN DEER

At the time of the White Dawn;
*   At the time of the White Dawn,*
I arose and went away.
*   At Blue Nightfall I went away.*

I ate the thornapple leaves
*   And the leaves made me dizzy.*
I drank the thornapple flowers
*   And the drink made me stagger.*

The hunter, Bow-Remaining,
*   He overtook and killed me,*
Cut and threw my horns away.
*   The hunter, Reed-Remaining,*
He overtook and killed me,
*   Cut and threw my feet away.*

Now the flies become crazy
*   And they drop with flapping wings.*
The drunken butterflies sit
*   With opening and shutting wings.*

Pima Indian

Dear Everybody,

The Goat Guys played at a club called The Vamp and we jammed. I wish you could have seen us. I made Raphael these cool fur pants so he really looks like a Goat Guy. It's getting warm and I'm having a little trouble concentrating on school. But don't worry. We're all doing our work and we only play in clubs on weekends mostly. Thanks for your letter.

Love,
Cherokee Goat-Bat

Horns

Cherokee noticed that the air was beginning to change, becoming powder-sugary with pollen as if invisible butterfly wings and flower petals were brushing against her skin. It was getting warmer. The light was different now—dappled greenish-gold and watery. After school, The Goat Guys would run, bicycle and roller-skate home to play basketball or, when Angel Juan got back from the restaurant wearing his white busboy shirt that smelled of soup and bread and tobacco, they would all ride to the beach in his red truck and surf or play volleyball on the sand until sunset. At night they rehearsed. It was hard for them to think about homework or studying when they were getting so many calls to play in clubs. Everyone wanted to see the wild goat singer, the winged witch drummer, the dark, graceful angel bass player and the spinning blonde tambourine dancer.

After rehearsals, or on weekends after the shows, Cherokee and Raphael stayed together in his bed or her tepee. She hardly slept. There was a constant tossing and tangling of their bodies, a constant burning heat. She remembered how she had slept before—a caterpillar in a cocoon, muffled and peaceful. Now she woke up fragile and shaky like some new butterfly whose wings are still translucent green, easy to tear and awaiting their color. All day she smelled Raphael on her skin. Her eyes were stinging and glazed and her head felt heavy. A slow ache spread through her hips and thighs.

"Cherokee and Raphael are doing it!" Witch Baby sang.

Cherokee tried to ignore her.

"Aren't you? Aren't you doing it?"

"Shut up, Witch."

"You are! I hear you guys. And you look all tired all the time."

"Stop it, Witch. You shouldn't talk. Why would you want to move out into the shed? I bet I know what you and Angel Juan do out there."

Witch Baby was quiet. She gnawed her finger-nails and pulled at a snarl-ball in her hair. Right away, Cherokee wished she hadn't said anything. She realized that Witch Baby wouldn't tease her if Witch and Angel Juan were doing the same thing.

Witch Baby bared her teeth at Cherokee. "I'm writing to Weetzie and telling!" she said as she roller-skated away.

Cherokee watched Angel Juan and Witch Baby more closely after that. She saw how Angel Juan tousled Witch Baby's hair and picked her up sometimes. But he did it like an older brother. When Witch Baby looked at Angel Juan, her tilty eyes turned the color of amethysts and got so big that her pointed face seemed smaller than ever.

One day, while The Goat Guys were rehearsing, Raphael went over and touched Cherokee's hair. It was only a light touch but it was so charged that tiny electric sparks seemed to flare up. Witch Baby stopped drumming. Angel Juan's eyes were hidden behind his sunglasses. Witch Baby looked at him. Then she got up and ran out of the room.

Cherokee followed her into the garden. "What is it, Witch?" she asked.

Witch Baby didn't answer.

"I see how he looks at you when you wear your wings and play drums for him. I think he's just afraid of his feelings."

Witch Baby shrugged and chewed her fingernails.

"Tell me about Angel Juan."

Witch Baby didn't say anything about Angel Juan out loud, but Cherokee could tell what she was thinking.

He is a dangerous flamenco shadow dancer and a tiny boy playing music in the gutter. His soul sounds like my drums and looks like doves. He is fireworks. He is the black-haired angel playing his bass on the top of the tree, on the top of the cake. I want him to see the flowers in my eyes and hear the songs in my hands.

After a show at The Vamp, some girls followed Raphael backstage. They wanted to stroke his fur pants, they told him, giggling. One kept flicking out her tongue like a snake. They wore black bras and black leather miniskirts.

Cherokee stood with her arms crossed on her chest, watching them. Then she noticed that Angel Juan was standing in the same position with a frown on his face that matched her own. He turned and stalked out of the club, and Witch Baby came and stood beside Cherokee.

"All the girls pay attention to Raphael but Angel Juan is a slinkster-cool bass player and beautiful, too," Cherokee said.

"Ever since you made Raphael those goat pants, he's been acting like the only person in the band," Witch Baby said. Then she added, "You never made anything for Angel Juan."

Cherokee wished the girls would leave Raphael alone, take their hands off his hips and their breasts away from his face. But she thought he was happier lately than he had ever been and he would hold her in the tepee that night and sing songs he had made up about her until the images of the girls drifted out of her head and she fell into a sleep of running animals and breaking lily-filled waves. But what about Witch Baby? She would be curled up in the shed under the bass drum, alone. She would dream of Angel Juan's obsidian hair and deer face, reach for him and find a hollow drum. What about Angel Juan? Cherokee thought. He would be waiting outside for them by his red truck with a frown on his face. He would drive home with swerves and startling stops. He would not look at any of them, especially Witch Baby. He was the only Goat Guy Cherokee had not made a present for.

What should I do for Angel Juan? Cherokee wondered. I will ask Coyote.

Cherokee, Witch Baby, and Raphael went out to meet Angel Juan at his truck.

"We were hot tonight," said Raphael.

Angel Juan turned to him. "What makes you think you are such a star all of a sudden, man?"

"I said *we*. I can't help it if the girls like me," Raphael said, tossing his dreadlocks back over his bare shoulders.

"They might like me too if I shook my hips at them like some stripper chick."

"Maybe they would." Raphael grinned and swiveled his hips in the goat pants. "Why don't you, man? Too freaked out?"

That was when Angel Juan made a fist and hit Raphael in the stomach under his ribs. Raphael staggered backward, staring at Angel Juan as if he weren't quite sure what had just happened.

Cherokee put her arms around Raphael. I will have to go back to Coyote, she thought.

Cherokee asked Coyote if she could go running with him around the lake. It was a morning of green mist, and needles of sun were coming through the pines. Cherokee had to run at her very fastest pace to keep up with Coyote's long legs. She glanced over at his profile—the proud nose, the flat dreamy eyelids, the trail of blue-black hair.

"Coyote . . ." Cherokee panted.

"We are running, Cherokee Bat," Coyote said. "Keep running. Think of making your legs long. Think of deer and wind."

When they had circled the lake twice, Cherokee leaned against a tree to catch her breath. She felt as if Coyote had been testing her, forcing her forward.

"Coyote," she said. "I have to ask you something."

Coyote was tall. He never smiled. He had chosen to live alone, to work and mourn and see visions, in a nest above the smog. The animals came to him when he spoke their names. He was full of grace, wisdom and mystery. He had seen his people die, wasted on their lost lands. Cherokee had never seen his tears but she thought they were probably like drops of turquoise or liquid silver, like tiny moons and stars showering from his eyes. She knew that he had more important things to do than give her gifts. But still, she needed him. And she had gone this far.

"Coyote, Angel Juan is jealous of Raphael. He's shy around girls—even Witch Baby, and I know he loves her. Witch Baby is jealous of how Raphael is with me. She wants Angel Juan to treat her the same way. Angel Juan is the only one of The Goat Guys I haven't made anything for," Cherokee blurted out. Then she stopped. Coyote was eyeing her.

"Cherokee Bat," he said. "The birds have given you feathers for Witch Baby. The goats have given you fur for Raphael Chong Jah-Love. What do you want now?"

"I want the horns on your shelf for Angel Juan," Cherokee whispered.

She was braced against the tree, and she realized that she was waiting for something, for thunder to crack suddenly or for the ground to shake. But nothing happened. The morning was quiet—the early sun coaxing the fragrance from the pines and the earth. Coyote did not even blink. He was silent for a while. Then he spoke.

"My people are great runners, Cherokee. They go on ritual runs. Before these they abstain from eating fatty meat and from sexual relations. These things can drain us."

Cherokee looked down at the ground and shrugged. "What do you mean?"

"You know what I mean. You are very young still. So is Raphael. Angel Juan and Witch Baby are both very young. You must be careful. While your parents are away, I am responsible. Use your wisest judgment and protect yourself."

"We do. I do," Cherokee said. "Weetzie told me and Witch Baby all about that stuff. But this is about Angel Juan. We all have what we want, but it's been harder for him his whole life and now he's the only one without a present."

177

"There is power, great power," Coyote said. "You do not understand it yet."

"I am careful," Cherokee insisted. "Besides, if I haven't been responsible, it doesn't have to do with you or with the wings and haunches. I just want the horns for Angel Juan so he won't feel left out."

"I cannot do any more for you. You'll have to make something else for Angel Juan. I cannot give you the horns."

"Coyote . . ."

"I want you to try to get more sleep," Coyote said. "If you want to find the trail, if you want to find your-self, you must explore your dreams alone. You must grow at a slow pace in a dark cocoon of loneliness so you can fly like wind, like wings, when you awaken."

I'm awake now, Cherokee wanted to shout. I'm a woman already and you want to keep me a child. You want us all to be children.

But instead she turned, jumped on Raphael's red bicycle and rode down the hill, away from the lake, away from Coyote.

Cherokee could not stop thinking about the horns. Why was Coyote so afraid of giving them to her? She had always known inside that the wings and the haunches were not just feathers and fur. The horns must have even greater power.

Cherokee rode home and found Witch Baby practicing her drums in the shed.

"I tried to get a present for Angel Juan," Cherokee said. "But Coyote won't help me. I don't know what to do."

"What about those goat horns you were talking about?"

Cherokee played with one of her braids. "Coyote said the horns have a lot of power. He's afraid to give them to us."

Witch Baby crunched up her face. "It's not fair. Coyote helped you get presents for me and Raphael." She was quiet for a moment. "I wonder what's so special about the horns," she said. "I want to find out."

"Witch, don't do anything creepy," Cherokee said. "Coyote is like a dad to us and he is very powerful."

Witch Baby pulled a tangle-ball out of her hair, looked at it and growled. Watching her, Cherokee wished she hadn't said anything about the horns.

Witch Baby might do something. But at the same time Cherokee was curious. What would happen to The Goat Guys if they had the magic horns?

I don't need to know, Cherokee told herself. I'll think of something else for Angel Juan. And Witch Baby is only a little girl. She won't be able to do anything Coyote doesn't want her to do.

Witch Baby was little. She was so small that she was able to slip in through the window of Coyote's shack one night. Witch Baby was very quiet when she wanted to be, and very fast—so quiet and fast that she was able to take the goat horns off a shelf and leave with them in her arms while Coyote slept. Witch Baby was very much in love. She had convinced Angel Juan to drive her up to Coyote's shack late at night and wait for her because, she said, Coyote had a present for them. Witch Baby was so in love that all she cared about was getting the horns. She didn't even think about how Coyote would feel when he woke a few moments after the red truck had disappeared down the hillside and saw that the familiar horn shadow was not falling across the floor in the moonlight.

When Witch Baby and Angel Juan got back to Witch Baby's house, they sat in the dark truck.

"Well, aren't you going to let me see?" Angel Juan asked.

Witch Baby took the horns out from under her jacket and gave them to him.

"Oopa! Brujita!"

"They're for you. I asked Coyote if I could have them for you."

Angel Juan held the horns up on his head and looked at himself in the rearview mirror. His eyes shone, darker than the lenses of the sunglasses he almost always wore.

"Thank you, Baby. This is the coolest present. I feel like a real Goat Guy now."

Witch Baby looked down to hide the flowers blooming in her eyes, the heat in her cheeks. Angel Juan leaned over and kissed her face. Bristling roughness and shivery softness, heat and cool, honeysuckle and tobacco and fresh bread and spring. The horns gleaming like huge teeth in Angel Juan's lap. Then Witch Baby leaped out of the car.

"Wait! Baby!" Angel Juan leaned his head out the

window of the truck and watched her run into the shed. The horns were cool, pale bone.

Angel Juan attached them to a headband so he could wear them when he played bass. The next night, backstage at The Vamp, he put them on and admired himself in the mirror. He looked taller, his chin more angular, and he thought he noticed a shadow of stubble beginning to grow there. He took off his sunglasses and turned to Witch Baby.

"Hey, what do you think?"

"You are a fine-looking Goat Guy, Angel Juan."

Cherokee and Raphael came through the door. Raphael and Angel Juan hadn't been speaking since the fight, but now, wearing his horns, Angel Juan forgot all about it. And Raphael was so impressed by the horns that he forgot too.

"Cool horns," he said, swinging his tail.

Cherokee gasped and pulled Witch Baby aside.

"What did you do?" She dug her nails into Witch Baby's arm. "Coyote will kill us!"

"Let go, clutch! I did it because I love Angel Juan. Just like you got goat pants for your boyfriend."

"I didn't go against anyone's rules."

"You and your stupid clutchy rules!"

"We have to give them back! Witch!"

Witch Baby jammed her hand into her mouth and began gnawing on her nails. Cherokee looked over at Angel Juan. He was very handsome with his crown of horns and he was smiling.

Maybe it would be okay just this once, Cherokee thought. We could play one show with the horns. Angel Juan would feel so good. And maybe the horns are really magical. Maybe something magical will happen.

Angel Juan was still showing Raphael the horns. He looked over at Witch Baby. "That niña bruja got them for me. Pretty good job, hey?" He grinned.

Cherokee sighed. "Listen, Witch," she whispered. "We'll play one gig with the horns and then we'll tell Angel Juan that Coyote has to have them back. We'll get him another present. But we can't keep them."

Witch Baby didn't say anything. It was time to go on.

If the crowd had loved The Goat Guys before, had loved the Rasta boy with animal legs, the drummer witch with wings and the dancing blur of blonde and fringe and beads that was Cherokee, then tonight they loved the angel with horns.

Angel Juan's horns glowed above everything, pulsing with ivory light. His body moved as if he were the music he played. When he slid to his knees and lifted his bass high, the veins in his arms and hands were full.

We are a heart, Cherokee thought.

After the set, she watched Angel Juan pick Witch Baby up in his arms and swing her around. Cherokee had never seen either of them look so happy. She hated to think about taking the horns back to Coyote.

But Angel Juan has the confidence he needs now even without the horns, she told herself. We all do.

So at dawn the next morning, Cherokee untangled herself from Raphael, crawled out of the tepee and tiptoed across the wet lawn to the garden shed. She saw Witch Baby and Angel Juan lying together on the floor, their dark hair and limbs merged so that she could not tell them apart. Only when they moved slightly could she see both faces, but even then they wore the same dreamy smile, so it was hard to tell the difference. Then Cherokee saw the horns gleaming in a corner of the shed. She lifted them carefully, wrapped them in a sheet and carried them away with her.

Cherokee got on Raphael's bicycle and started to ride to Coyote's shack. But at the foot of Coyote's hill Cherokee stopped. She took the horns from the basket on the front of the bicycle and stroked them, feeling the weight, the smooth planes, the rough ridges, the sharp tips. She thought of last night on stage, the audience gazing up at The Goat Guys, hundreds of faces like frenzied lovers. It had never been like that before. She thought of the witch and angel twins, wrapped deep in the same dream on the floor of the garden shed.

Cherokee did not ride up the hill to Coyote's shack. Goat Guys, she whispered, turning the bike around. Beatles, Doors, Pistols, Goat Guys.

When Cherokee got home, the horns weighing heavy in the basket on the front of Raphael's bicycle, the sun had started to burn through the gray. Some flies were buzzing around the trash cans no one had remembered to take in.

Cherokee felt sweat pouring down the sides of her body and the sound of Raphael's guitar pounded in her head as she walked up the path.

Witch Baby was waiting in the living room eating Fig Newtons. She glared at Cherokee. "Where are they?"

Cherokee handed over the horns. Then she turned and went to her tepee, pulled the blanket over her head and fell asleep.

The wind blew a storm of feathers into her mouth, up her nostrils. Goats came trampling over the earth, stirring up clouds of dust. Horns of white flame sprang from their heads. And in the waves of a dark dream-sea floated chunks of bone, odd-shaped pieces with clefts in them like hooves.

At the next Goat Guy show, the band came on stage with their wings, their haunches, their horns. The audience swooned at their feet.

Cherokee spun and spun until she was dizzy, until she was not sure anymore if she or the stage was in motion.

Afterward two girls in lingerie and over-the-knee

leather boots offered a joint to Raphael and Angel Juan. All four of them were smoking backstage when Cherokee and Witch Baby came through the door.

Witch Baby went and wriggled onto Angel Juan's lap. He was wearing the horns and massaging his temples. His face looked constricted with pain until he inhaled the smoke from the joint.

"Are you okay?" Witch Baby asked.

"My head's killing me."

Angel Juan offered the burning paper to Witch Baby. She inhaled, coughed and gave it to Raphael, who also took a hit.

"Want a hit, Kee?" he asked.

The girls in boots looked at each other, their lips curling back over their teeth.

"No thanks," Cherokee said. She went and stood next to Raphael and began playing with his hair.

The girls in boots crossed and uncrossed their legs, then stood up.

"We'll see you guys later," said one, looking straight at Raphael. The other smiled her snarl at Angel Juan. Then they left.

"Ick! Nasty!" Witch Baby hissed after them.

"I saw that one girl in some video at The Vamp," said Raphael. "She had cow's blood all over her. It was pretty sick." He took another hit from the joint and gave it back to Angel Juan.

"Let's get out of here," Cherokee said, wrinkling her nose at the burned smell in the air.

But the next time Raphael offered her a joint, she smoked it with him. The fire in her throat sent smoke signals to her brain in the shapes of birds and flowers. She leaned back against his chest and watched the windows glow.

"Square moons," she murmured. "New moons. Get it? New-shaped moon."

Later, in the dark kitchen, lit only by the luminous refrigerator frost, they ate chocolate chip ice cream out of the carton and each other's mouths.

But in the morning Cherokee's throat burned and her chest ached, dry. There were no more birds or flowers or window-moons, and when she tried to kiss Raphael he turned away from her.

The band played more and more shows. Cherokee's skull was full of music, even when it was quiet. Smoke made her chest heave when she tried to run. She remembered drinks and matches and eyes and mouths and breasts coming at her out of the darkness. She remembered brushing against Witch Baby's wings, feeling the stage shake as Raphael galloped across it; she remembered the shadow of horns on the wall behind them and Angel Juan massaging his temples. When she woke in the morning, she felt as if she had been dancing through her sleep, as if she had been awake in the minds of an audience whose dreams would not let her rest. And she did not want any of it to stop.

Some days, Angel Juan would drive Cherokee, Raphael and Witch Baby to school and then go to work. But more and more often they all just stayed home, piled in Weetzie's bed, watching soap operas and rented movies, eating tortilla chips and talking about ideas for new songs. At night they came to life, lighting up the house with red bulbs, listening to music, drinking beers, taking hot tubs on the deck by candlelight, dressing for the shows. At night they were vibrant—perfectly played instruments.

Sometimes Cherokee wanted to write to her family or visit Coyote, but she decided she was too tired, she would do it later, her head ached now. They would be out of school soon anyway, so what did it matter if they missed a few extra days, she told herself, running her hands over Raphael's thigh in the haunch pants. And they were doing something important. Lulu from The Vamp had told Raphael that she thought they could be the next hot new band.

Angel Juan and Witch Baby were kissing on the carpet. Through the open windows, the evening smelled like summer. It would be night soon. There would be feathers, fur and bone.

OMEN

By daylight a fire fell. Three stars together it seemed: flaming, bearing tails. Out of the west it came, falling in a rain of sparks, running to east. The people saw, and screamed with a noise like the shaking of bells.

Aztec Indian

Dear Everybody,

    I know the film is very important but sometimes I wish you were home. Maybe The Goat Guys can be in your next movie.

                                            Love,
                                            Cherokee

Hooves

Summer came and the canyon where Cherokee lived smelled of fires. Sometimes, when she stood on the roof looking over the trees and smog and listening to the sirens, she saw ash in the air like torn gray flesh. She wond   what Coyote was thinking as the hills burned around him. If lines had formed in his face when he had discovered that the horns were gone. Lines like scars. She had not spoken to him in weeks.

That summer there was dry fragile earth and burning weeds, buzzing electric wires, parched horns and the thought of Coyote's anger-scars. There was Cherokee's reflection in the mirror—powder-pale, her body narrow in the tight dresses she had started to wear. And there were the shows almost every night.

The shows were the only things that seemed to matter now. More and more people came, and when Cherokee whirled for them she forgot the heat that had kept her in a stupor all day, forgot the nightmares she had been having, the charred smell in the air and what Coyote was thinking. People were watching her, moving with her, hypnotized. And she was rippling and flashing above them. On stage she was the fire.

And then one night, after a show, The Goat Guys came home and saw the package at the front door.

"It says 'For Cherokee.'"

Witch Baby handed over the tall box and Cherokee took it in her arms. At first she thought it was from her family. They were thinking of her. But then she saw the unfamiliar scrawl and she hesitated.

"Open it!" said Angel Juan.

"You have a fan, I guess," said Raphael.

Cherokee did not want to open the box. She sat staring at it.

"Go on!"

Finally, she tore at the tape with her nails, opened the flaps, and removed the brown packing paper. Inside was another box. And inside that were the hooves.

They were boots, really. But the toes were curved, with clefts running down the front, and the platform heels were sharp wedges chiseled into the shape of animal hooves. They were made of something fibrous and tough. They looked almost too real.

"Now Cherokee will look like a Goat Guy too!" Angel Juan said.

"Totally cool!" Raphael picked up one of the boots. "I wish I had some like this!"

Cherokee sniffed. The hooves smelled like an animal. They bristled with tiny hairs.

"Put them on!"

She took off her moccasins and slid her feet into the boots. They made her tall; her legs were long like the legs of lean, muscled models who came to see The Goat Guys play. She walked around the room, balancing on the hooves.

"They are hot!" Raphael said, watching her.

They were fire. She was fire. She was thunderbird. Red hawk. Yellow dandelion. Storming the stage on long legs, on the feet of a horse child, wild deer, goat girl . . .

"Cherokee! Cherokee!"

They were calling her but she wasn't really listening. She was dancing, thrusting. Her voice was bells. Her tambourine sent off sparks. The Vamp audience reached for her, there at the bottom of the stage, there, beneath her hooves.

She spun and spun. She had imagined she was the color of red flame but she was whiter than ever, like the hottest part of the fire before it burns itself out.

Later, someone was reaching down her shirt. She called for Raphael but he was not there. Witch Baby came and pulled her away. Feathers were flying in a whirlwind. Her feet were blistering inside the hoof boots.

Then they were back at the house. Raphael had invited Lulu over and he, Lulu and Angel Juan were on the couch sharing a joint. Candles were burning. Raphael touched Lulu's smooth, dark cheek with the back of his hand. Or had Cherokee imagined that? Her feet hurt so much and in the candlelight she could have been mistaken.

"Help me take these off," she said to Witch Baby. "Please. They hurt."

Witch Baby pulled at one boot. Every part of her body strained, even the tendons in her neck. Finally she fell backward and Cherokee's foot was free, throbbing with pain. Witch Baby pulled on the other boot until it came off too.

"It cut me! Nasty thing!"

"What?"

"Your boot cut me." There was blood on Witch Baby's hand.

"Let's wash it off."

They went into the bathroom and Cherokee held on to the claw-footed tub for balance. She felt as if she were going to be sick and took a deep breath. Then she helped clean the cut that ran across Witch Baby's palm like a red lifeline.

"I want to stop, Witch Baby," she whispered.

Witch Baby stood at the sink, her wings drooping with sweat and filth, her eyes glazed, blood from her hand dripping into the basin. "Tell that to our boyfriends out there on the couch," she said. "Tell that to Angel Juan's horns."

But what did Angel Juan's horns tell Angel Juan?

The next night The Goat Guys smoked and drank

tequila before the show. On stage they were all in a frenzy. Cherokee, burning with tequila, could not stop whirling, although her toes were screaming, smashed into the hooves. Witch Baby was playing so hard that the wings seemed to be flapping by themselves, ready to fly away with her. Raphael leaped up and down as if the fur pants were scalding him. Finally, he leaped into the audience and the people held him up, grabbing at matted fur, at his long dreadlocks, at his skin slippery with sweat.

While Raphael was thrashing around in the audience trying not to lose hold of his microphone, Angel Juan pumped his bass, charging forward with his whole body like a bull in a ring. He swung his head back and forth as if it were very heavy, crammed full of pain and sound. He slid to his knees. Something flashed in his hand. Cherokee thought she could hear the audience salivating as they yelled. They saw the knife before she did. They saw Angel Juan make the slash marks across his bare chest like a warrior painting himself before the fight. They reached out, hoping to feel his blood splash on them.

It was only surface cuts; The Goat Guys saw that

later when they were at home cleaning him. But Cherokee's hands were trembling and her stomach felt as if she had eaten a live thing. She took the horns off Angel Juan's head.

He sat in a chair, his eyes half closed. Witch Baby was kneeling at his feet with a reddened washcloth in her hands. Raphael stood by himself, smoking a cigarette. They all watched Cherokee as she put the horns on the floor and backed away from them.

"We have to give them back to Coyote," she said.

"What are you talking about?"

"The horns. They don't belong to us. Coyote was here while we were out." Cherokee reached into her pocket and held out three glossy feathers she had found tied to the front door. "We have to give back the horns."

"You can't do that now," Witch Baby said. "Tomorrow night we'll have at least two record companies at our house! We need the horns!"

"Yeah, Cherokee, cool out," Angel Juan said. "You're just uptight about tomorrow."

"Look at you!" She pointed to his chest.

"He's all right. Lots of rock stars get carried away

and do stuff like that. And we won't drink anything tomorrow," Raphael promised her.

She wanted him to hold her but lately they almost never touched. After the shows they were always too exhausted to make love and collapsed together, chilled from their sweat and smelling of cigarettes, when they got back.

"And we're not even playing at a club. It'll be like my birthday party," Witch Baby said.

"Better! We're so much hotter now. Bob Marley, Jimi Hendrix, Jim Morrison, Elvis."

"I'm not doing any more shows 'til we give back the horns," Cherokee said. "Don't you see? We have to stop!"

"Don't worry," Raphael said. "Coyote gave us the horns. Why are you so afraid?"

Witch Baby began gnawing her cuticles, her eyes darting from Cherokee to Raphael. When Cherokee saw her, she just shook her head silently at Raphael. She couldn't tell him and Angel Juan the truth about the horns because she was afraid they wouldn't be able to forgive her and Witch Baby for what they had done.

When she fell asleep that night, Cherokee dreamed she was in a cage. It was littered with bones.

The night of the party, the house was crammed with people. They wore black leather and fur and drank tall, fluorescent-colored drinks. Some were in the bedrooms snorting piles of cocaine off mirrors. They were playing with the film equipment, pretending to surf on the surfboards, trying on beaded dresses and top hats, undressing the Barbie dolls and twisting the Mexican skeleton dolls' limbs together. There were some six-foot-tall models with bare breasts and necklaces made of teeth. Men with tattooed chests and scarred arms. The air was hot with bodies and smoke.

Before The Goat Guys played live, Raphael put on their tape—his own loping, reggae rap, Angel Juan's salsa-influenced bass, Witch Baby's rock-and-roll-slam drums, Cherokee's shimmery tambourine and backup vocals. A few people were dancing, doing the "goat." They rocked and hip-hopped in circles, butting each other with imaginary horns.

Cherokee was drinking from a bottle of whiskey

someone had handed her when she saw Lulu go over to Raphael. Lulu was wearing a very short, low-cut black dress, and she leaned forward as she spoke to him. Cherokee could not hear what they were saying, but she saw Raphael staring down Lulu's dress, saw Lulu take his hand and lead him away. On the stereo, Raphael's voice was singing.

"White Dawn," Raphael sang. It was a song he had written when the band first started, a name he never used anymore.

Cherokee followed Raphael and Lulu into Weetzie's bedroom. She watched Lulu bend her head, as if she were admiring her reflection in a lake, and inhale the white powder off a mirror. She watched Raphael stand and flex his bare muscles. Lulu put her hands on Raphael's hips.

That was when Cherokee turned and ran out of the room.

First, she found Raphael's haunches lying in her closet. The hot, heavy fur scratched her arms when she lifted the pants. Next, she found Angel Juan's horns and Witch Baby's wings strewn on the floor of the living room among the bottles and cigarette butts, dolls, surf equipment and cannisters of film. Cherokee was already wearing the hooves.

She took the armload of fur and bone into the bathroom, pulled off her clothes, and stared at her reflection—a weak, pale girl, the shadows of her ribs showing bluish through her skin like an X ray.

I am getting whiter and whiter, she thought. Maybe I'll fade all the way.

But the hooves and haunches and horns and wings were not fragile. Everything about them was dark and full, even the fragrance that rose from them like the ghosts of the animals to whom they had once belonged. Cherokee had seen her friends transformed by these things, one at a time. She had seen Witch Baby soar, Raphael charge, Angel Juan glow. She had felt the wild pull of the hooves on her feet and legs. But what would it be like to wear all this power at once, Cherokee wondered. What creature could she become? What music would come from her, from her little white-girl body, when that body was something entirely different? How would they look at her then, all of them, those faces below her? How would Raphael look at her, how would his eyes shine, mirrors for her alone? He would look at her.

Cherokee stepped into the haunches. They made her legs feel heavy, dense with strength. Her feet in the boots stuck out from the bottom of the hairy pants as if both hooves and haunches were really part of her body. She fastened Witch Baby's wings to her shoulders and moved her shoulder blades together so that the wings stirred. Then she attached Angel Juan's horns to her head. In the mirror she saw a wild creature, a myth-beast, a sphinx. She shut her eyes, threw back her head and licked her lips.

I can do anything now, Cherokee thought, leaving the bathroom, passing among the people who had taken over the house so that she hardly recognized it anymore. Angel Juan was on the couch, surrounded by girls, their limbs flailing, but Cherokee didn't see Witch Baby anywhere.

Then Cherokee passed the room where Raphael and Lulu were sitting on the bed, staring at each other. Raphael did not take his eyes off Lulu as Cherokee walked by.

I don't need Raphael or Weetzie or Coyote or anybody, Cherokee told herself. She kept her eyes focused straight ahead of her and paraded like a run-way model.

Cherokee climbed up the narrow staircase and out onto the roof deck, into the night. She could see the city below, shimmering beyond the dark canyon. Each of those lights was someone's window, each an eye that would see her someday and fill with desire and awe. Maybe tonight. Maybe tonight each of those people would gaze up at her, at this creature she had become, and applaud. And she wouldn't have to feel alone. Even without her family and Coyote. Even without the rest of The Goat Guys. Even without Raphael. She would fly above them on the wings she had made.

Cherokee swayed at the edge of the roof, gazing into the buoyant darkness. She felt the boots blistering her feet, the haunches scratching her legs, the horns pressing against her temples; but the wings, quivering with a slight breeze, would lift her away from all that, from anything that hurt. The way they had lifted Witch Baby from the mud.

Cherokee spread out her arms, poised.

And that was when she felt flight. But it was not the flight she had imagined.

Something had swept her away but it was not the wings carrying her into air. Something warm and steady and strong had swept her to itself. Something with a heartbeat and a scent of sage smoke. She was greeted, but not by an audience of anonymous lights, voices echoing her name. She recognized the voice that drew her close. It was Coyote's voice.

"Cherokee, my little one," Coyote wept. They were not the tears of silver—moons and stars—she had once imagined, but wet and salt as they fell from his eyes onto her face.

DREAM SONG

Where will you and I sleep?
At the down-turned jagged rim of the sky
you and I will sleep.

Wintu Indian

Dear Cherokee, Witch Baby, Raphael
and Angel Juan,

We are coming home.

> *Love,*
> *Weetzie*

Home

The first things Cherokee saw when she woke were the stained-glass roses and irises blossoming with sun. Then she shifted her head on the pillow and saw Raphael kneeling beside her.

"How are you feeling?" he whispered, his eyes on her face.

She nodded, trying to swallow as her throat swelled with tears.

"We're all going to take care of you."

"What about you?"

"Don't worry, Kee. Coyote said he is going to help all of us. I'm going to quit drinking and smoking, even. And he called Weetzie. They're all on their way home."

"What about Angel Juan's headaches?"

"Coyote is going to get some medicine together." He pressed his forehead to her chest, listening for her heart. "I'm so sorry, Cherokee."

"I just missed you so much."

"Me too. Where were we?"

Cherokee looked down at herself, small and white beneath the blankets. "Do you like me like this?" she asked. The tears in her throat had started to show in her eyes. "I mean, not all dressed up. I'm not like Lulu. . . ."

Raphael flung his arms around her and she saw the sobs shudder through his back as she stroked his head. "You are my beauty, White Dawn."

Coyote, Witch Baby and Angel Juan came in with strawberries, cornmeal pancakes, maple syrup and bunches of real roses and irises that looked like the windows come to life. They gathered around the bed scanning Cherokee's face, the way Raphael had done, to see if she was all right.

"What happened?" Cherokee asked them.

"Witch Baby saw how you were acting at the party and she went to get Coyote," Angel Juan said, squinting and rubbing his temples.

"She told me all about the horns," Coyote said. "Forgive me, Cherokee."

"*I'm* sorry," Cherokee said. "About the horns."

"It's my fault!" said Witch Baby. "I should never have taken those clutch horns."

"Yes," said Coyote, "we were all at fault. But I am supposed to care for you and I failed."

"Did you know we had the horns?" Cherokee asked.

"I could have guessed. I turned my mind away from you. Sometimes, there on the hilltop, I forget life. Dreaming of past sorrows and the injured earth, I forget my friends and their children who are also my friends."

"What are we going to do?"

"I called your parents and they will be home in a few days."

"But will you help us now?" Cherokee asked. She looked over at Witch Baby, who was gazing at Angel Juan as if her head ached too. "Will you help take away Angel Juan's headaches and help Raphael stop smoking?"

The lines running through Coyote's face like scars were not from anger but concern. He took Cherokee's cold, damp hands in his own that were dry and warm, solid as desert rock. "I will help you," Coyote said.

After they had scrubbed the house clean, glued the broken bowls, washed the salsa- and liquor-stained tablecloths, waxed the scratched surfboards, and fastened the dolls' limbs back on, Coyote, Cherokee, Raphael, Witch Baby and Angel Juan gathered in a circle on Coyote's hill.

Coyote lit candles and burned sage. In the center of the circle he put the tattered wings, haunches, horns and hooves. Then he began to chant and to beat a small drum with his flat, heavy palms.

"This is the healing circle," Coyote said. "First we will all say our names so that our ancestor spirits will come and join us."

"Angel Juan Perez."

"Witch Baby Wigg Bat."

"Raphael Chong Jah-Love."

"Cherokee Bat."

"Coyote Dream Song."

Coyote Dream Song chanted again. His voice filled the evening like the candlelight, like the smoke from the sage, like the beat of his heart.

"Now we will dance the sacred dances," Coyote said, and everyone stood, shyly at first, with their hands in their pockets or folded on their chests. Coyote jumped into the air as he played his drum, and the music moved in all of them until they were jumping too, leaping as high as they could. Then Coyote began to spin and they spun with him, circles making a circle, planets in orbit, everything becoming a blur of fragrant shadow and fragmented light around them.

"And we will dance our animal spirit," Coyote said, crouching, hunching his shoulders, his eyes flashing, his face becoming lean and secretive. The circle changed, then. There were ravens flying, deer prancing, obsidian elks dreaming.

Finally, the dancing ended and they sat, exhausted, leaning against each other, protected by ancestors who had recognized their names, and glowing with the dream of the feathers and fur they might have been or would become.

"This is the healing circle," Coyote said. "So you may each say what it is you wish to heal. Or you may think it in silence." And he put his hand to his heart, then reached to the sky, then touched his heart again.

"The children in my country who beg in gutters and the hurt I gave to Witch Baby," Angel Juan said.

"My Angel Juan's headaches and all broken hearts," Witch Baby said.

"Cherokee's blistered feet and anything in the world that makes her sad," Raphael murmured.

"Our damaged earth. Angel Juan's headaches. Raphael's desire for smoke. Witch Baby's sweet heart. Cherokee's pain," Coyote said.

Wings, haunches, horns and hooves, thought Cherokee Bat. Wings, haunches, horns, hooves, home. Then, "All of you," she said aloud.

Coyote put his hand to his heart, reached to the sky, then touched his heart again.

That was when the wind came, a hot desert wind, a salt crystal wind, ragged with traveling, full of memories. It was wild like the wind that had brought Cherokee the feathers for Witch Baby's wings, but this time there were no feathers. This wind came empty, ready to take back. Cherokee imagined it extending cloud fingers toward them, toward the circle on the hill, imagined the crystalline gaze of the wind when it recognized Witch Baby's wings made from the feathers it had once brought.

The wings also recognized the wind and began to flap as if they were attached to a weak angel crouched in the center of the circle. They flapped and flapped until they began to rise, staggering back and forth in the dust. Cherokee, Raphael, Witch Baby, Angel Juan and Coyote stared in silence as the wind reclaimed the wings and carried them off, flapping weakly into the evening sky.

Witch Baby stood and reached above her head, watching the wings disappear. Then she collapsed against Angel Juan and he held her.

"You don't need them," he whispered. "You make me feel like I have wings when you touch me." And as he spoke, one fragile feather, glinting with a streak of green, drifted down from the sky and landed upright in Witch Baby's hair.

Meanwhile, Raphael was inching toward the haunches that lay in front of him. Cherokee could see by his eyes that he wasn't sure if he was ready to give them up. But it was too late.

The goat had come down the hill. One old goat

with white foamy fur and wet eyes. Unlike the goats who had come before, to give their fur to Coyote and Cherokee, this goat was quiet, so quiet that when he had gone, dragging the haunches in his mouth, Coyote and The Goat Guys were not sure if he had been there at all. Raphael started to stand, but Cherokee touched his wrist. He reached for her hand and they turned to see the goat being swallowed up by the hillside, a wave vanishing back into the ocean.

Cherokee knew what she had to do. Coyote was standing, facing her with a shovel in each hand. He held one out. Together, Cherokee and Coyote began to dig a hole in the dirt in the center of the circle. Dust clouds rose, glowing pink as the sun set, and the pink dust filled Cherokee's eyes and mouth.

The hooves were much heavier than they looked, heavier, even, than Cherokee remembered them, and the bristles poked out, grazing her bare arms. The hooves smelled bad, ancient, bitter. She dropped them into their grave. Then she and Coyote filled the grave up with earth and patted the earth with their palms. The dust settled, the sun slipped away, darkness eased over everything.

Coyote built a fire on the earth where the hooves were buried. The flames were dancers on a stage, swooning with their own beauty.

Angel Juan was staring into these flames. His horns lay at the edge of the fire and Cherokee remembered her dream of flame horns springing from goat foreheads. She watched Angel Juan stand and pick up the horns. Then Coyote held out his arms and Angel Juan went to him, placing the horns in Coyote's hands. Coyote set the horns down in the fire and embraced Angel Juan. Like a little boy who has not seen his father in many years, Angel Juan buried his head against Coyote's chest. All the pride and strength in his slim shoulders seemed to fall away as Coyote held him. When he moved back to sit beside Witch Baby, his forehead was smooth, no longer strained with the weight or the memory of the horns.

Later, after Cherokee, Raphael, Witch Baby and Angel Juan had left, looking like children who have played all day in the sea and eaten sandy fruit in the sun and gone home sleepy and warm and safe; later, when the fire had gone out, Coyote took the horns from the log ashes and brushed them off. Then Coyote

Dream Song carried the horns back inside.

When Cherokee and Raphael got back to the canyon house, they set up the tepee on the grass and crept inside it. They lay on their backs, not touching, looking at the leaf shadows flickering on the canvas, and trying to identify the flowers they smelled in the warm air.

"Honeysuckle."

"Orange blossom."

"Rose."

"The sea."

"The sea! That doesn't count!"

"I smell it like it's growing in the yard."

They giggled the way they used to when they were very young. Then they were quiet. Raphael sat up and took Cherokee's feet in his hands.

"Do they still hurt?" he asked, stroking them tenderly. He moved his hands up over her whole body, as if he were painting her, bringing color into her white skin. As if he were playing her—his guitar. And all the hurt seemed to float out of her like music.

They woke in the morning curled together.

"Remember how when we were really little we

used to have the same dreams?" Cherokee whispered.

"It was like going on trips together."

"It stopped when we started making love."

"I know."

"But last night . . ."

"Orchards of hawks and apricots," Raphael said, remembering.

"Sheer pink-and-gold cliffs."

"The sky's wings."

"The night beasts run beside us, not afraid. Dream-horses carry us . . ."

"To the sea," they said together as they heard a car pull into the driveway and their parents' voices calling their names.

At the end of the summer, The Goat Guys set up their instruments on the redwood stage their families had helped them build behind the canyon house. Thick sticks of incense burned and paper lanterns shone in the trees like huge white cocoons full of electric butterflies. A picnic of salsa, home-baked bread still steaming in its crust, hibiscus lemonade and cake decorated with fresh flowers was spread on the lawn. Summer had ripened to its fullest—a fruit ready to drop, leaving the autumn tree glowing faint amber with its memory as the band played on the stage for their families and friends.

Cherokee looked at the rest of The Goat Guys playing their instruments beside her. Even dressed in jeans and T-shirts, Raphael and Angel Juan could pout and gallop and butt the air. Witch Baby seemed to hover, gossamer, above her seat. The music moved like a running creature, like a creature of flight, and Cherokee followed it with her mind. She was a pale, thin girl without any outer layers of fur or bone or feathers to protect or carry her. But she could dance and sing, there, on the stage. She could send her rhythms into the canyon.

Francesca Lia Block

is the acclaimed author of the *Los Angeles Times* best-sellers GUARDING THE MOON: *A Mother's First Year*, THE ROSE AND THE BEAST, V T & CLAIRE, and DANGEROUS ANGELS: *The Weetzie Bat Books*; as well as BEAUTIFUL BOYS, WASTELAND, ECHO, I WAS A TEENAGE FAIRY, GIRL GODDESS #9: *Nine Stories*, and THE HANGED MAN. Her work is published around the world.